WHAT PROGRAMS DO YOU NEED?

Most projects in this book can be carried out using the kinds of programs that you probably already have on your computer. The instructions are aimed at personal computer users with *Microsoft® Windows® 95* and *Microsoft® Office* installed on their computer. Details of any additional programs needed are given in the relevant sections.

Microsoft® Windows® 95 includes several useful programs such as Paint and WordPad.

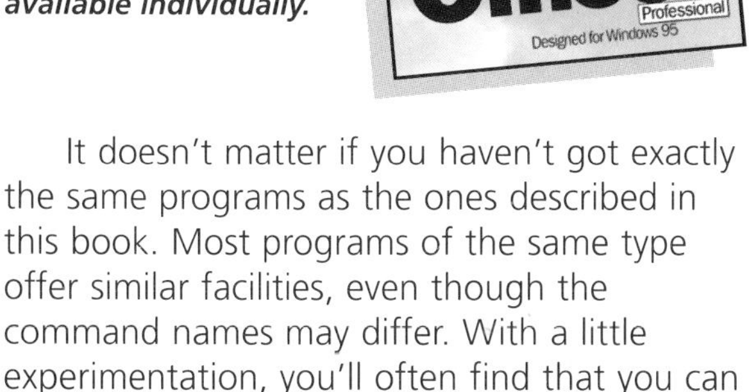

Microsoft® Office is a collection of programs which includes Excel, Access, Word, Powerpoint and Schedule+. These programs are also available individually.

It doesn't matter if you haven't got exactly the same programs as the ones described in this book. Most programs of the same type offer similar facilities, even though the command names may differ. With a little experimentation, you'll often find that you can achieve the same effects.

Throughout the book there are references to places on the Internet where you can obtain programs, some of which are free. You can also turn to pages 60 to 62 for advice on alternative programs that you can buy.

WHAT EQUIPMENT DO YOU NEED?

If you have a multimedia computer like the one shown below, you will be able to carry out the projects in this book that involve working with sound. Otherwise, you can add extra equipment to your computer, so that it is capable of producing sounds.

A multimedia computer

For some projects, you'll need access to the Internet. For this, you need a device called a modem and an account with a company called an Internet service provider. You can find out more information about the programs and equipment you need on pages 60 to 62.

If there's anything your computer doesn't have, don't worry. You'll still be able to do many of the projects in this book. Then, if your school or one of your friends has a computer with the right equipment, perhaps you could try out the other projects on their computer.

INTERNET TIPS

The Internet is changing all the time. New information is added and old information is removed. If you can't find some of the information referred to in this book, it could be because it's no longer there. If you turn to project 71, you can find out how you can search for up-to-date material.

This section contains ideas for things to draw and make using your computer. The instructions given are for the *Paint* program supplied with *Windows® 95*. But many of the projects will work just as well with other drawing and painting programs.

1 DRAW IN BLACK AND WHITE

Colour pictures drawn on a computer may not print out well in black and white. If you don't have a colour printer, change your palette to a black and white one, like the one below. These simple shades look very effective. Because they print out as they appear on the screen, you'll know exactly what to expect.

A black and white palette

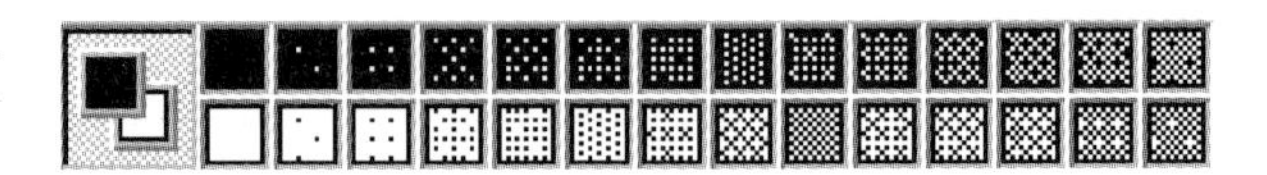

To paint in black and white, choose *Attributes* from the *Image* menu in *Paint*. In the *Colors* section of the dialog box, select *Black and White* and then click on *OK*. Use a mixture of dark and light shading to create contrast in your picture.

2 MAKE PICTURES FROM SHAPES

You can use shape tools to help you to sketch basic outlines for your pictures. You could just use the *Brush* or *Pencil* tools, but it's easier to create neat shapes using shape tools than to draw them free-hand using a mouse.

Try using the *Ellipse* tool to draw a pig. Click and drag to make a big oval shape for the body. Then add a smaller circle on top for the head. To draw a perfect circle, hold down the Shift key on your keyboard as you drag. Once you have an outline for your picture, you can then use the other tools to add more detail.

A pig shape drawn using the Ellipse tool

Use the Curve Line tool to draw a mouth.

Use the Polygon tool to add legs.

3 PAINT A FUZZY SCENE

It can be difficult to draw good pictures on your computer using a mouse. But your pictures don't have to contain lots of realistic detail. Try using *Paint's Airbrush* tool. It creates a fuzzy effect, like spray paint, so you don't need to be as accurate as you do when you're using other tools. It's great for effects like smoke, clouds or treetops.

A fuzzy scene made using the Airbrush tool

USBORNE COMPUTER GUIDES

101 THINGS TO DO WITH YOUR COMPUTER

Gillian Doherty

Edited by Philippa Wingate

Designed and illustrated by Griff

Cover design: Russell Punter
Additional designs: Michèle Busby, Susannah Owen, Rachel Kirkland, Rachel Wells, Michael Wheatley

Photography: Howard Allman
Technical consultant: Michael Sullivan Internet consultant: Thomas Barry
Managing editor: Jane Chisholm Managing designer: Stephen Wright

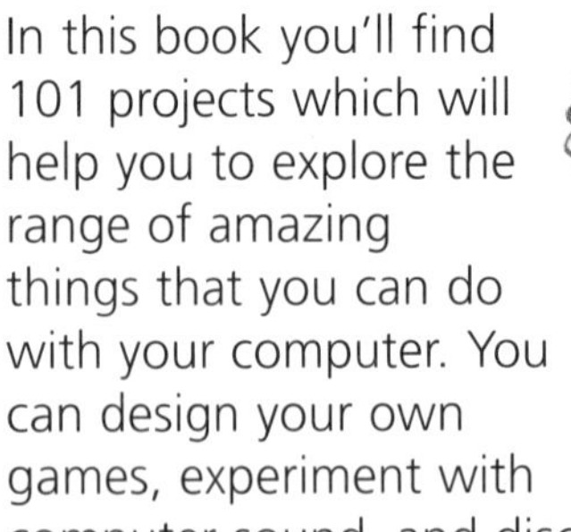

In this book you'll find 101 projects which will help you to explore the range of amazing things that you can do with your computer. You can design your own games, experiment with computer sound, and discover what the Internet has to offer. Each project will help you to learn new skills and explore the programs and facilities on your computer.

You could use the project ideas in this book as a starting point to help you develop your own ideas and investigate the areas of computing that you find most interesting.

READING THIS BOOK

In general, the projects at the beginning of the book are easier than the ones towards the end. The earlier projects also require programs and equipment that are less specialized.

The projects are grouped together in sections, according to the program used to create them, or the skills and techniques that they explore. You don't have to work through them in the order they are listed, but you may find it easier to do so. If you do decide to dip into different parts of the book, you will be directed to projects which describe relevant techniques when appropriate.

It's a good idea to read the introduction at the beginning of each section. This gives general information about the projects in that section and the programs you need to use to carry them out.

For some projects, there are detailed instructions which you will need to follow very carefully. For others, the information is more general and may build upon skills you already have. If you need any extra guidance, you could use the *Help* menu in the relevant program to look up the information you need.

4 MAKE FUNNY FACES

You can make funny pictures by stretching a picture to distort its shape. Try drawing a self-portrait using a black outline on a white background. Save and name your "ordinary" picture.

Click on the *Selection* tool and drag a frame around the picture. Then select *Stretch/Skew* from the *Image* menu. Try stretching the figure horizontally by 200%.

An ordinary picture

You can stretch a figure horizontally...or vertically.

Now try distorting sections of the face. For example, select the mouth area and stretch it horizontally. Then drag it to the position you want. Try out some of the other commands on the *Image* menu to see what effect they have.

When you have finished distorting an image, shade it in and save it. Save each version with a different name.

Distort different parts of the face and move them around.

5 ADD DEPTH TO PICTURES

Give a picture a realistic 3D effect by building it up layer-by-layer. Unlike ordinary paints, computer paints don't blur together when you try to paint over them. So you can keep adding extra bits to a picture without making a mess. Make the objects on each layer a little larger than on the previous layer, so that they seem closer to you.

These pictures show how to build up a jungle scene layer-by-layer.

Draw the background first. ***Put some animals in the picture.*** ***Add bushes in front of the animals.*** ***Make the figures at the front large.***

6 DECORATE TEXT

Add a stylish touch to text by decorating basic letter shapes with patterns and pictures.

Add bright patterns to liven up text.

In *Paint,* select the *Text* tool. Open the *Text Toolbar* from the *View* menu and choose a font style and a large font size (48 points or more). Select a colour for your text by clicking on the colour you want on the palette. Click in the text box you have created and type your name. Drag the blocks, or "handles", of the text box if you need more space.

Change the shape of a letter by adding bits to it.

When you have finished typing, click outside the text box. The text is now part of the picture. You can no longer change the wording of the text, but you can alter it in the ways that you can alter a picture, for example by erasing bits or adding bits to it.

Select the *Magnifier* tool. Below the *Tool Box*, you will see the values 1x, 2x, 6x and 8x. Select 8x to zoom in on part of a letter, ready to start decorating. To change the colour of individual letters, select the *Fill* tool and choose a colour from the palette. Click within the edges of a letter to fill it with colour. Use the drawing and shape tools to add more intricate patterns and pictures.

You can use these techniques to design unusual text for badges or elaborate headings.

You could use the letter shape as the basis for a picture.

7 ADD SHADOWS

Create an eerie effect by adding mysterious shadows to your *Paint* pictures.

Draw a spaceship outline in the top half of the drawing area, or canvas. Use the *Free-Form Select* tool to cut round it and then select *Copy* from the *Edit* menu. Select *Paste* from the *Edit* menu to create a copy of it.

To turn the copy upside down, click on *Flip/Rotate* on the *Image* menu. Select *Flip vertical* and click on *OK*. Then drag the upside-down image to directly below the original picture.

If there are any gaps in the outline of the copy, you will need to patch them up using the *Pencil* tool. Then use the *Fill* tool to shade it black or grey. Finally, add colour and detail to the original spaceship. When you have finished, it will look as though it is casting a shadow.

You can produce different kinds of shadow by stretching and slanting an image. Use the same technique as above to copy the image. Then, instead of flipping the copy, select *Stretch/Skew* on the *Image* menu. Try stretching your image in different ways and at different angles. Shade in the shadow in the same way as above.

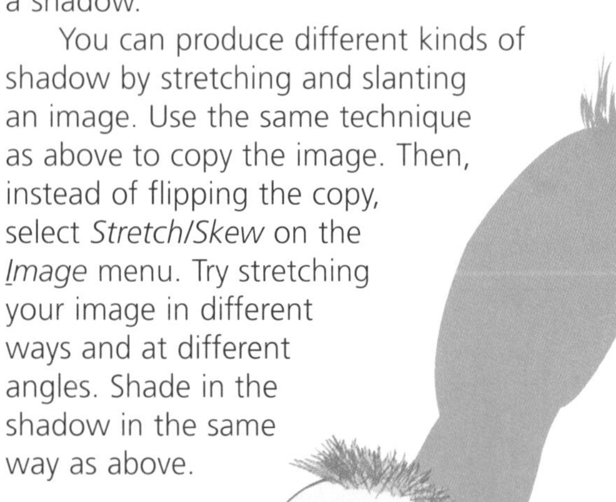

These shadows were skewed horizontally and stretched vertically.

8 DESIGN A PERSONAL SYMBOL

Design a tiny picture to use as your personal symbol on letters, envelopes or cards. Your personal symbol should remind people of you. So try to think of a hobby or interest that your friends would associate with you, and then design a symbol based on it. For example, if you are interested in music, you could draw musical notes or headphones.

In *Paint*, select *Attributes* from the *Image* menu and make your canvas 3cm high and 3cm wide. Select the *Magnifier* tool and click on 8x in the box below the tool box to zoom in on the canvas. Use simple shapes for your symbol. Fine detail won't show up when it is viewed at the right size. To see what your symbol looks like at the actual size, select the *Magnifier* tool and click on 1x. When you have finished, select *Save As* from the *File* menu and name your picture **Symbol.bmp**.

Some ideas for symbols

9 MAKE PERSONAL CARDS

Print out handy cards containing your name and address so that you can easily pass your details on to friends.

Select *Attributes* from *Paint's Image* menu and create a canvas 8.5cm wide and 5.5cm high. Use the *Rectangle* tool to draw a rectangle that fills the canvas. This makes a card that should fit neatly in your wallet.

You could insert a personal symbol (see project 8). To do this, select *Paste From* on the *Edit* menu. Find and select **Symbol.bmp** and click on *Open* to insert it. Then drag the picture to the position you want on the canvas.

Use the *Text* tool (see project 6) to type in your name and address. Drag the text box into place and then add any extra decoration.

When you have finished, select the card and click on *Copy* on the *Edit* menu. Change the size of the canvas to 21cm wide and 29.5cm high. Then use the *Paste* command on the *Edit* menu to make several copies of the card on one canvas. Print out the canvas on ordinary paper. Then glue the print-out to a piece of thin card. When the glue is dry, use scissors to cut out each card.

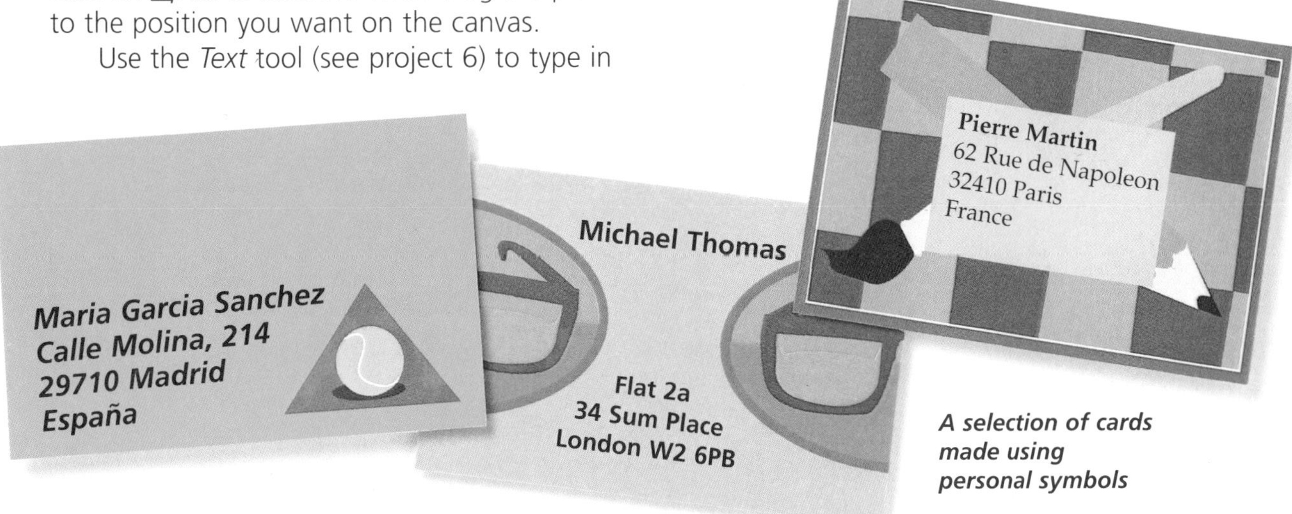

A selection of cards made using personal symbols

10 SPOT THE DIFFERENCE

Make a game to puzzle your friends by drawing two pictures that are almost identical, and asking them to spot the differences.

In *Paint,* create a canvas 12cm wide and 10cm high. Use the *Rectangle* tool to draw a box that almost fills the canvas. Then use your drawing and painting tools to create a picture with lots of detail. When you have finished, select *Save As* and name the file **Spot1.bmp**.

Now make ten changes to the picture. You could alter the colour of someone's clothes using the *Fill* tool, add something extra, such as a flower in a buttonhole, or rub something out using the *Eraser* tool. Save the changed picture with the name **Spot2.bmp**.

Can you find ten differences between these pictures?

Print out the pictures and see whether your friends can find all the differences. If you don't have a colour printer, leave the pictures as outlines and then shade in the print-out. If you do shade them yourself, take care not to add extra differences without meaning to.

11 WRAP UP A PRESENT

It's easy to print out attractive tags to attach to birthday gifts. In *Paint*, create a canvas 7cm wide and 5cm high. This will be your gift tag. Decorate the tag with a simple pattern or picture.

Then select the *Ellipse* tool. Holding down the Shift key, draw a small circle in the top left corner of the canvas, about 1cm from the edge. Use the *Print* command on the *File* menu to print out your canvas.

Glue the print-out onto thin card and use scissors to cut round the gift tag. Use a hole-punch to make a hole where the circle is.

You could even make matching wrapping paper using the copying technique described in project 9. To do this, create a large canvas. Then select and copy your gift tag design and paste lots of copies of it onto the canvas.

Print your own gift tags and matching wrapping paper.

PRINTING TIPS

If you don't have a colour printer, you could use the black and white shading technique described in project 1. Alternatively, just use simple outlines and then decorate your print-out with pens or paints.

12 PERSONALIZE A CARD

Mark a friend's birthday or achievement by sending a card with a personal message.

In *Paint,* create a canvas 12cm wide and 17cm high. Draw a picture to go on the front of the card. Make sure you leave space for a short message at the top or bottom of the canvas. Then use the *Text* tool to add a greeting to the front of the card (see project 6 for advice on using the *Text* tool). You could include the name of the person you are sending it to as part of the greeting.

Print out the picture. Then fold a piece of thin, coloured card (24cm wide and 17cm high) in half and glue your print-out to the front.

A personalized greetings card

13 MAKE A CHAIN CARD

Make a fun card made from a chain of dancing clowns. In *Paint,* start with a canvas 5cm wide and 11cm high. Draw a picture of a clown, making sure his hands and feet touch the sides of the canvas. Select the clown and then click on *Copy* on the *Edit* menu. Change the canvas width to 10cm and select *Paste* from the *Edit* menu to copy the clown.

With the copied clown still selected, click on *Flip/Rotate* on the *Image* menu. Select *Flip horizontal* and click on *OK*. The copy will be flipped over. Move it beside the first clown to make it look as though they are holding hands.

Once again, choose *Select All* from the *Edit* menu and select *Copy.* Change the canvas width to 20cm. Paste the clowns and flip them over as before. Drag them beside the first two. You can add more clowns, but the more you add the more difficult they will be to cut out.

Draw a rectangular outline that fills the canvas. Print out the picture and cut out the canvas. Fold the paper as shown on the right, and cut out the clowns.

Cut through all the folds of paper at once.

14 DESIGN TEAM T-SHIRTS

You can use *Paint* to design T-shirts for the sports team you play for.

Create a canvas 10cm wide and 15cm high. Leaving a space at the bottom for the team name, draw a simple picture that will remind people of the name. For example, American football teams such as the *Miami Dolphins* and the *Chicago Bears* have animals in their names and logos. Or, your picture could represent the sport you play. For example, you could draw a football, or a basketball net.

Use the *Text* tool (see project 6) to type in your team's name. Position it below the picture. You could personalize shirts by adding players' names or numbers. To do this, save the basic T-shirt design and then add the name or number to it. Save each design with a different name.

There are lots of shops that will copy pictures onto T-shirts. To do this with your design, first you need to print it out onto paper. Then take your print-out to a shop that offers a printing service. Ask them to enlarge the design so that it fills the T-shirt.

15 MAKE A CARD GAME

Design and print your own cards to play a game of "pairs". The object of the game is to spot when two matching cards appear.

In *Paint,* create a canvas 6.5cm wide and 9cm high. Use the *Rectangle* tool to draw a rectangular outline that almost fills the canvas. This is your card shape. Use the *Fill* tool to shade it in. Click on the *Selection* tool and select the card. Then select *Copy* from the *Edit* menu. Change the size of the canvas to 20.5cm wide and 29cm high and select *Paste* from the *Edit* menu. A copy of the card will appear. Drag it beside the first one. Select *Paste* again to create more copies.

Draw a different design on each card. You could base your designs on a particular theme, such as fish with different patterns, or faces with different expressions. When you have filled a canvas, save it and create a new one. You should design around 20 different cards. Then print out two copies of each canvas. Glue each canvas to a sheet of thin card and cut out the playing cards.

To play the game, deal out all of the cards face down. Players shouldn't look at their cards. Each player in turn places a card face-up on a pile on the table. When you see an identical pair of cards placed one on top of the other, shout "snap" and place your hand over the matching cards. The first player to do this takes the cards that have been played in that round and adds them to his or her pile. This person starts the next round. The overall winner is the person who wins all of the cards.

Watch carefully for the matching pairs.

16 ARRANGE A SCREEN COLLAGE

Build up an unusual collage made from images collected from the Internet or from the programs on your computer.

You can copy a picture from your computer screen, called taking a screen grab, and then use it as part of a *Paint* picture. To do this, press the Print Screen key (or Alt and Print Screen) on your keyboard. Launch *Paint* and select *Paste* from the *Edit* menu. A message may appear telling you that the image is too large and asking whether you want the bitmap enlarged. If it does, click on *Yes*. After a short time, your screen grab will appear in the *Paint* window.

Use the *Free-Form Select* tool to cut out the section of the image you want to use. Open a second *Paint* window by launching the program from the *Start* menu. Then select *Paste* from the new window's *Edit* menu. Use this window to arrange a selection of images in an interesting way. You can then use the *Paint* tools to edit the picture and add extra details.

Most images in your computer programs and on the Internet are protected by copyright. This means that a company or person owns them. You should write to the copyright owner to ask for permission before you use them for something public such as a school magazine.

A selection of pictures arranged in a collage

17 PRINT A TAPE COVER

Print out unique covers for any loose cassette tapes in your music collection, or for recordings you've made yourself.

In *Paint,* create a canvas 2.5cm wide and 10cm high. Select the *Line* tool. Holding down the Shift key on your keyboard, draw a vertical line along the right-hand edge of the canvas. Change the width of the canvas to 3.8cm and draw a second line along the new edge. Then alter the canvas width to 10.3cm.

Select the *Rectangle* tool and draw a rectangular outline that fills the canvas. The large section on the right of the canvas will be the front cover. Use the Text tool (see project 6) to type the name of the band and the title of the recording here. Draw a picture to go with it.

To add the title to the "spine" of the cover, select *Flip/Rotate* from the *Image* menu and click on *Rotate by angle* and *270°*. Select the *Text* tool and type the title in the middle section of the canvas. Then print out your design and cut it out. Fold creases along the inner lines and place the cover in a tape case.

Print out lively covers for your tapes or CDs.

18 MAKE A FLIP BOOK

You can animate a simple picture by making a flip book. Flip books are made from lots of pages, each showing the same picture in a slightly different position. When you flick through the pages quickly, the picture looks as though it is moving.

Try making a simple flip book showing a bouncing ball. Select *Attributes* from *Paint's Image* menu and create a canvas 8cm wide and 6cm high. Draw a rectangle that fills the canvas. This will be one page of your flip book. Draw a ball in the top right corner of the rectangle. (Only use the right-hand edge, as this will be the part you see when you flick through the flip book.) Select the rectangle area which represents your page and click on *Copy* on the *Edit* menu. Change the size of the canvas to 20.5cm wide and 29cm high.

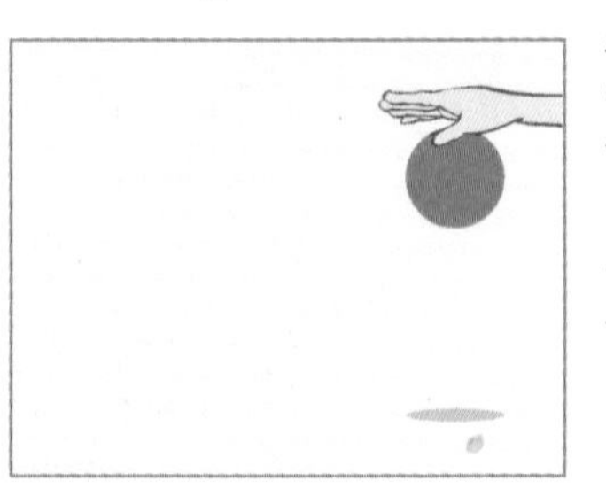

The first page of the book

Add detail to the picture to make it more interesting.

Select *Paste* from the *Edit* menu. Then drag the copy so that it's below the original page. This will be the second page of the flip book. On this page, use the *Free-Form Select* tool to cut out the ball. Then move the ball down slightly.

Repeat this technique to add more pages. Don't forget to move the ball down on each page. When the ball reaches the bottom of the page, start to move it up again.

The more pages a flip book has, the better the animation will look. A good flip book needs at least 16 pages. You can fit 8 pages onto an A4 canvas.

Print out each canvas onto an A4 sheet of paper. Cut out the individual pages of the flip book. Stack them in the order in which they were created, with the first page at the bottom. Staple, or clip, the pages together at the left-hand side.

Now flip through the book from back to front to see your ball bounce.

Here's another idea for a flip book. Change the position of the frog's legs on each page, to make it look as though it's jumping.

19 LEAVE A PICTURE TRAIL

In *Paint*, there is a way of dragging an image so that it leaves a trail of copies of itself. To try out this technique, draw a very simple picture. Make the outline of the picture black and the background white. Leave lots of space around it.

Use the *Free-Form Select* tool to cut round your picture.

A simple picture trail can make an effective border.

Then, holding down your left mouse button and the Shift key on your keyboard, drag the selected image. The image will leave a picture trail.

If you want more control over where the image is copied, hold down the Control key as you drag. Each time you release the left mouse button, a copy of the image will appear.

When you have finished, you can shade in the picture and add extra details.

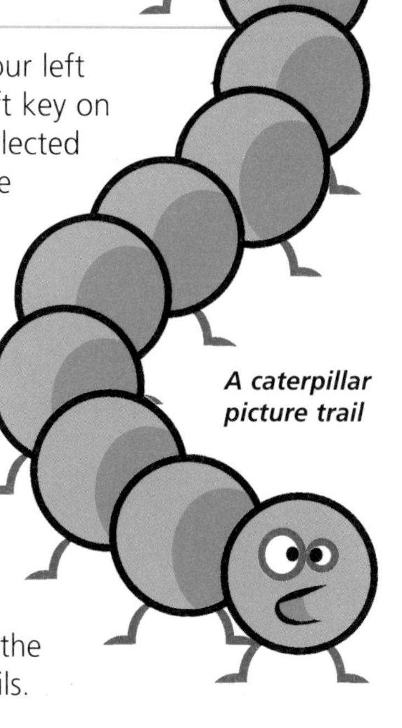

A caterpillar picture trail

20 DESIGN A CARTOON STRIP

Draw your own cartoon strip, using pictures to tell a simple story. First, think of a story that can be told in three or four pictures. For example, the cartoon below shows somebody shooting at a target. In the final picture, or frame, you see what he has actually hit. Each frame tells a bit more of the story.

Use a similar background in each frame. Instead of redrawing it, select some or all of the basic background and use the Copy and Paste commands on the *Edit* menu to copy it. Place the frames side by side to form a "strip".

Now you need to add the story details. Rub out any bits you want to change using the *Eraser* tool. Then use the *Magnifier* tool to zoom right in to add new details. You could use the *Text* tool to add captions, or to put text in speech bubbles. To do this, open the *Text Toolbar* from the *Image* menu and select a font size that will fit neatly.

Use the Ellipse tool to create speech bubbles.

When you have finished, print out your cartoon strip. You could even add it to a newspaper design (see project 27).

Tell a story in pictures.

You use a word-processing program to type in and arrange text. In these projects, you can find out about some of the useful and creative things that a word-processing program enables you to do with text. *Windows® 95* has a simple program called *WordPad,* which you can use for most of the projects in this section. But for some projects, you will need a more advanced program, such as *Microsoft® Word.*

21 MAKE TEXT SMILE

Smilies, or emoticons, are funny little faces made from the letters and symbols on your keyboard. People often use them in e-mails (see project 81). They help to indicate the tone of a message and show how you are feeling, so that people know when you're happy or sad, angry or amused. Here are some examples of smilies. You need to turn the page sideways to see them properly.

:-) Happy

:-(Sad

:-o Surprised

:-D Laughing

:-/ Not sure

]:-[Angry

s:-] Elvis

;-(Crying

Try inventing some smilies of your own. You can use any word-processing program to do this. Select New on the File menu to create a new document and then start typing. Think carefully about how the letters and symbols will look when viewed sideways. Which would work well as the mouth or the eyes? You can use your smilies in any text document, even in a printed letter.

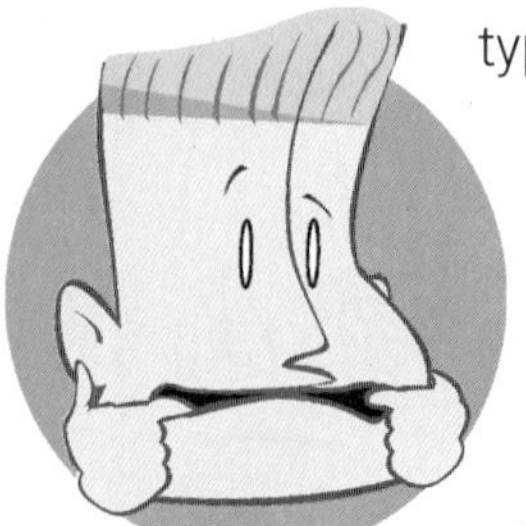

22 TYPE A PICTURE

If you don't have a drawing or painting program on your computer, you can make interesting pictures using text.

Sketch a simple line drawing onto a sheet of graph paper, as shown on the right. Then shade in each square that the line passes through. This is the basic shape that you will use to create your text picture.

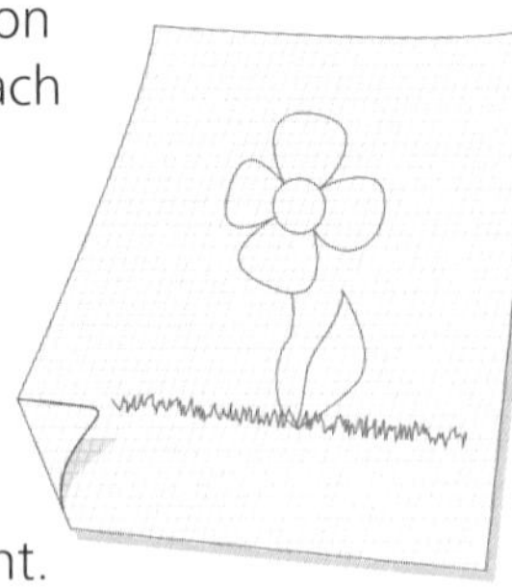

Launch your word-processing program and create a new document. Select a "standard" font (see project 23), for example *Courier*. Then recreate your picture on the screen, using text to replace the shaded squares. Start at the top left-hand side of the grid. If a square is blank, press the spacebar on your keyboard. If it is shaded, press a letter or symbol. Press the Return key when you get to the end of each line.

Use different letters and symbols to vary the textures in your picture. You could even use the letters that make up your picture to spell out a hidden message.

```
              mmmmm
            mmmmmmmm
           mmmmmmmmn
            mmmmmmmm
      mmm     m. . . . m
   mmmmmm . .  . . . . mmmmmm.
 n mmmmm . . . . . .  mmmmmmm.
  mmmmmm . . . . . . mmmmmmm
            mmm . . .mmmmmmm
           mmmmmm
          mmmmmmm
           mmmmm
             mmm
               H
               e          w
               l         ww
               l         www
                o       wwww
                f      wwwww
                 r    wwww
                  i  ww
                   end
MMMMMMMMMMMMMMMMMMMMMMMMMMMMMMMMM
```

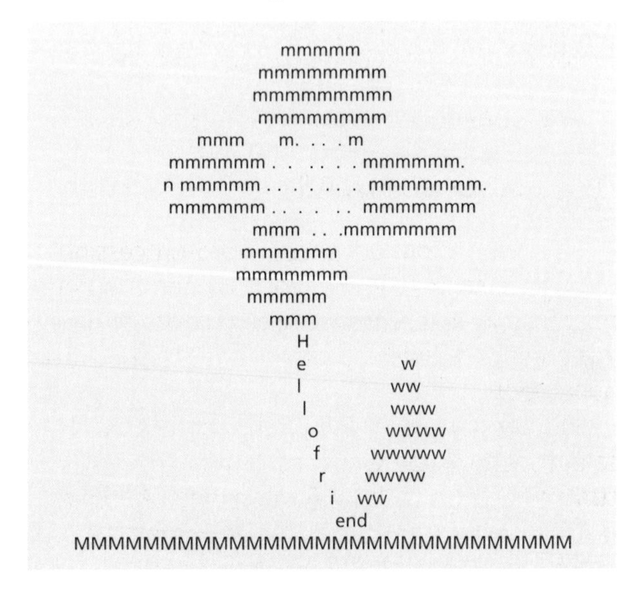

Can you spot the hidden message in this picture?

23 PRINT OUT NOTICES

You can use any word-processing program to print out neat, bold notices to pin to doors or noticeboards. If you are using *WordPad,* create a new document and then select *Page Setup* from the *File* menu. Select the paper size you want to use to print out your notice from the drop-down list.

Type in the text for your notice. You can alter the appearance of the characters that make up your text by changing the font. First, you need to select the text you want to change. To do this, click in front of the first word you want to select. Then hold down the left mouse button and drag the mouse to highlight the text. Select *Font* from the *Format* menu and choose the name of a font from the drop-down list. The *Sample* box shows what it will look like. You can also select a font size. Click on *OK* when you have found the size and style you want.

Part of the Font dialog box

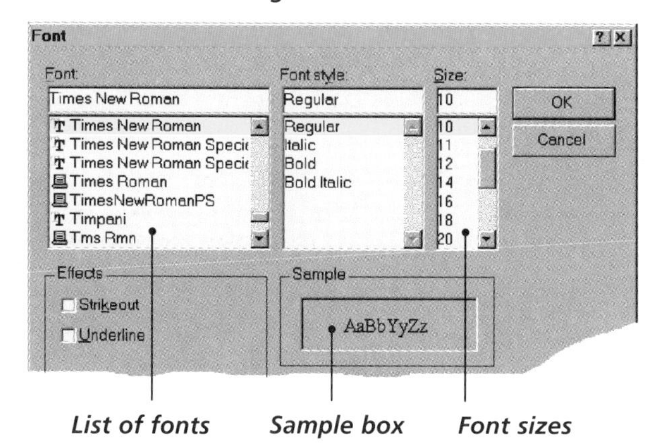

You can <u>underline</u> text, make it **bold**, or put it in *italics*. To do this, select the words you want to change and click on the relevant button on the *Format bar.* (You may need to switch this on from the *View* menu.) To switch a style off, select the text and click on the button again.

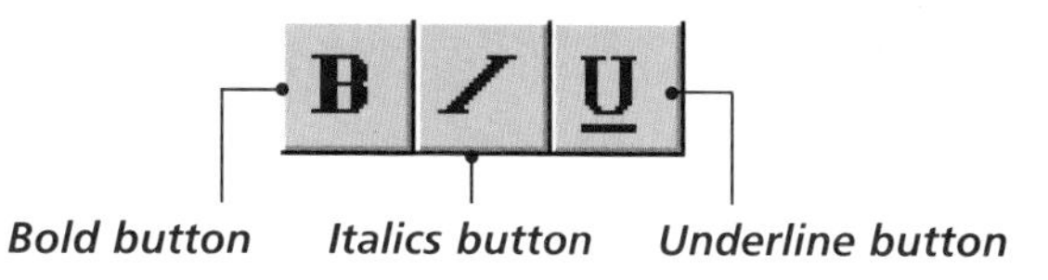

To position your text in the middle of the page, select it and click on the *Center* button.

Center button

Before you print your notice, select *Print Preview* from the *File* menu to check that it looks right. If it does, click on *Print* to enter your printer details. Then click on *OK* to print it out.

24 ADD BORDERS

With more advanced word-processing programs, such as *Word,* you can add a border to surround text. These simple frames can give a professional finish to labels, notices and other documents.

To add a border to a paragraph of text, first select the text you want the border to surround. Then click on *Borders and Shading* on the *Format* menu. Select the *Borders* tab and choose the *Box* option in the *Presets* section. Choose a style from the *Style* list and select a colour for the border from the box below it. You can specify the space you want to leave between the text and the border in the *From Text* box. When you have finished, click on *OK* to make the border appear around your text.

25 DESIGN A LETTERHEAD

Don't waste time writing your address at the top of every letter you write. Instead, design a letterhead document that you can use over and over again.

Launch *WordPad* and create a new document. Type in your address. Choose a font for the text using the method described in project 23.

To position the address in the middle of the page, select the text and click on the *Center* button (see project 23). Or, for a traditional letter layout, position the address in the top right-hand corner of the document, with a neat left-hand edge. To do this, select the address and click on the *Ruler* at the point where you want the left edge of the text to line up. (You may need to switch on the *Ruler* on the *View* menu.) An L-shaped symbol will appear. To make the text line up with the symbol, position the cursor at the beginning of each line of your address in turn, and press the Tab key on your keyboard. The text will then move into position.

The text lines up below the L-shaped symbol.

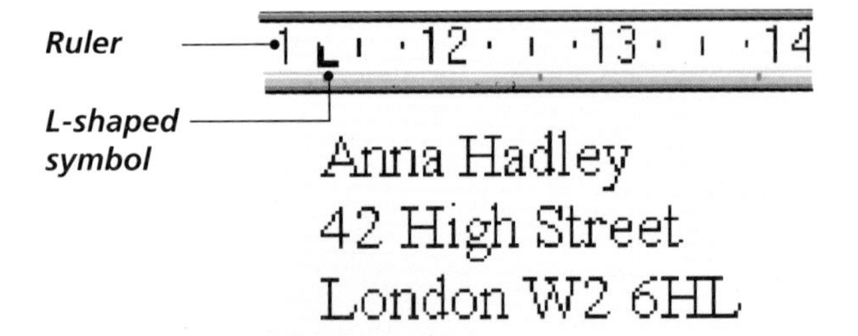

When you have finished designing your letterhead, select *Save As* from the *File* menu and save it with the name **Letter.doc**. Now whenever you want to write a letter, just open this document and type it in. Save your finished letter with a different name. Otherwise, the new document will replace the old one.

26 ADD PICTURES TO DOCUMENTS

It's easy to add a picture drawn using *Paint* to a text document. You could make bright, personalized notepaper by adding a picture to a letterhead (see project 25). But first you need to draw a picture and save it. Look at pages 4 to 13 for ideas.

Open the document that you want to add a picture to. Position the cursor where you want it to appear. In *WordPad,* it's easiest to insert the picture on a line without any text. Then select *Object* from the *Insert* menu.

To insert your picture, select *Create from File* and click on the *Browse* button. Find and select the picture file and click on the *Insert* button. Make sure the *Display As Icon* box is not selected and then click on *OK* to add the picture to your document.

Click on the picture to select it. A frame will appear around it. You can change the shape of the picture by dragging the blocks, called handles, in the frame. This will also distort the picture.

A selected picture appears in a frame.

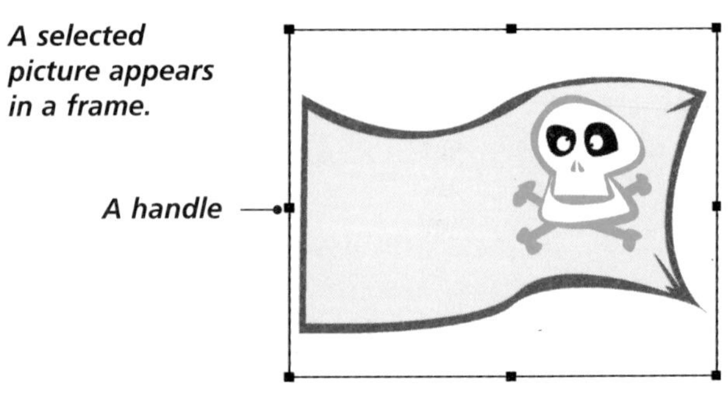

27 PRINT A NEWSPAPER

Some of the more advanced word-processing programs, such as *Word,* allow you to arrange text in columns, as it is in newspapers. You could write a school newspaper and use this technique to give it a professional look. Or, you could produce a joke newsletter about your friends, writing it in the style of a tabloid newspaper, with outrageous headlines.

Create a new document. Select *Page Layout* from the *View* menu. Then click on the *Columns* button on the *Standard Toolbar*. You can arrange your text in up to four columns. Click on the option you want. For example, to put your text into three columns, click on the third column.

Columns button options

Click here to create three columns.

Now type in the text for your articles. Make the headlines big and bold. (Find out how to change the font type and size in project 23.) You could even add pictures, using the method described in project 26.

As you type, you'll notice that when the text reaches the bottom of one column, it automatically continues at the top of the next one. If you want to make an article begin at the top of a new column, position the cursor at the end of the previous article and select *Break* from the *Insert* menu. Select the *Column Break* option and click on *OK*.

You can also vary the numbers of columns in different areas of the page. Simply select the section of text you want to work with. Then click on the *Columns* button and choose the number of columns you want to divide it into. If you want a heading to span all the columns, first select it. Then click on the *Columns* button and choose one column.

You can arrange your newspaper in columns like this.

The Daily News

6 October

My sister is an alien!

Residents of Little Hollow were still in shock today, following allegations by a ten-year-old local boy that his sister is an alien.

In an exclusive interview with The Daily News, Harry Thomas tells his extraordinary story. Harry made his claim after his sister refused to help him with his homework, but denies suggestions

You can insert a file, such as a *Paint* picture or a text document, into a *WordPad* document so that it only appears as an icon. (This works with any file created by a program that uses a system called Object Linking and Embedding.) When you double-click on the icon, the file will open. You can use this technique to create lots of unusual projects.

28 MAKE A JOKE BOOK

It's important that the punchline to a joke is a surprise. In printed joke books, you often see punchlines at the bottom of the page, or you have to turn to the back of the book to read them. An on-screen joke book is much better. To read the punchline, you just need to double-click on an icon when you're ready.

Create a new document in *WordPad* and type in a joke. Then create a second *WordPad* document and type in the punchline. Save and name each document. Open the first document and position your cursor where you want the punchline file's icon to appear. Select *Object* from the *Insert* menu. In the box that appears, select *Create from File*. Find and select your punchline file. Then make sure *Display As Icon* is selected and click on *OK*. An icon will appear in your document. Now, when someone has read the joke and is ready for the punchline, all they have to do is double-click on its icon and the punchline will appear.

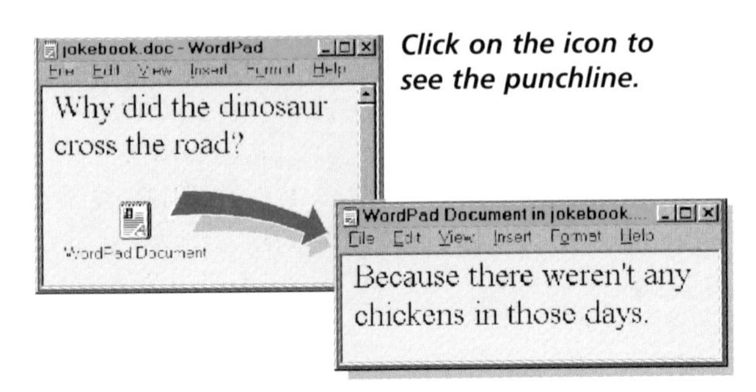

Click on the icon to see the punchline.

29 WRITE AN INTERACTIVE STORY

Use your imagination to invent an interactive story where a reader can choose from lots of different alternatives to determine what happens next in the plot. Look at the example below to see how this works.

Arrange your story in sections of one or two sentences. Each section should develop the story. Create a *WordPad* document and name it **story1.doc**. In this document, type in the beginning of your story. At the end of this, you should give two possible courses of action for the reader to choose from. Then create two new *WordPad* documents (**story2.doc** and **story3.doc**) which tell the next stage of the story for each of these possibilities. Insert these documents (see project 28) into **story1.doc** beside the section that they follow on from.

Then, in each of these two documents, give more plot possibilities and add more files to develop these options. You'll need to plan your story very carefully.

The icon you choose determines what happens next.

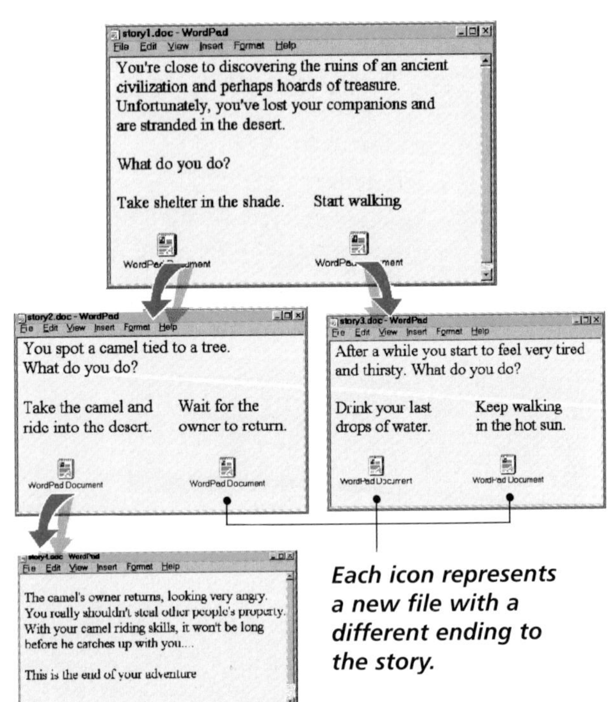

Each icon represents a new file with a different ending to the story.

30 SEND A SECRET MESSAGE

Write a letter to a friend containing a secret message hidden in a picture. Launch *WordPad* and create a new document. Type your secret letter and save and name it. Create a second document containing your ordinary letter. Then use *Paint* to draw a picture. This will be used to disguise the secret message.

Use the *Selection* tool to select the picture and click on *Copy* on the *Edit* menu. Open your ordinary letter and position your cursor where you want the picture to appear. Select *Object* from the *Insert* menu. Then select *Package* from the *Object Type* list and click on *OK*. An *Object Packager* window will appear.

An Object Packager window

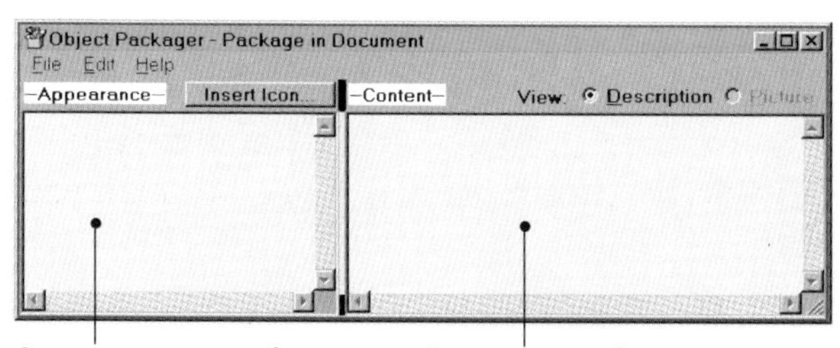

Appearance section ***Content section***

In the *Object Packager* window, select the word *Appearance* above the left-hand section. Then click on *Paste* on the *Edit* menu to paste your picture into that section. Select the word *Content,* above the right-hand section. Then click on *Import* on the *File* menu. Find and select your hidden message file and click on *Open.* To add the packaged file to your document, select *Update* from the *File* menu.

Copy the letter file onto a floppy disk and give it to a friend. To read the secret message, they just need to double-click on the picture.

The picture hides another message.

31 TRANSFORM A PICTURE

You can set up a picture that can be transformed simply by double-clicking. Launch *Paint* and draw "before" and "after" pictures similar to the ones below. The second picture could be a development of the first one. Save and name both pictures.

Before and after clicking

Open the first picture file and use the *Selection* tool to select it. Then click on *Copy* on the *Edit* menu. Create a new document in *WordPad.* Launch *Object Packager* and paste your picture into the *Appearance* section, using the technique described in project 30. Then select the *Content* section in *Object Packager* and click on *Import* on the *File* menu. Find and select the name of your second picture and click on *Open.* Select *Update* from the *File* menu to add the package to the document. Your first picture will appear in the document. When you double-click on it, a *Paint* window will appear showing the second one. As with project 30, you can copy your file onto a floppy disk to send to a friend.

32 INVENT AN ON-SCREEN GAME

You can invent a simple game, like a board game, that can be played on your computer screen. To construct a display like the one below, you'll need to use an advanced word-processing program. This one was created using *Microsoft® Word 7.0*. To play the game, you'll need a dice to roll. Launch *Paint* and create a background picture for the game. It could be based around a theme, such as an island adventure or a battle scene. Don't include position squares (see picture below); you'll add these later. When you have finished, select the picture and click on *Copy* on the *Edit* menu.

Launch *Word* and create a new document. Select *Paste* from the *Edit* menu to paste in the picture. Select *Toolbars* from the *View* menu and make sure *Drawing* is selected.

Fill tool

To add position squares, select the *Fill* tool to choose a colour for the squares. Select the *Text Box* tool and click and drag to draw each square.

Text Box tool

Next you need to add the game details. For some squares, you could simply click on them and type an instruction such as "Miss a go" or "Go back 3". In others, you could insert hidden documents containing a selection of questions. If a question is answered correctly, the player receives an extra turn. Use the technique described in project 30 to package the documents, drawing a small icon such as a question mark to represent each file.

To play the game, begin on the Start square. Use the *Ellipse* tool to create counters. Select the Fill tool to choose a different colour for each one. Players take turns to roll the dice and then move the relevant number of squares by dragging their counter. To win, you must reach the Finish square first.

Ellipse tool

An on-screen game

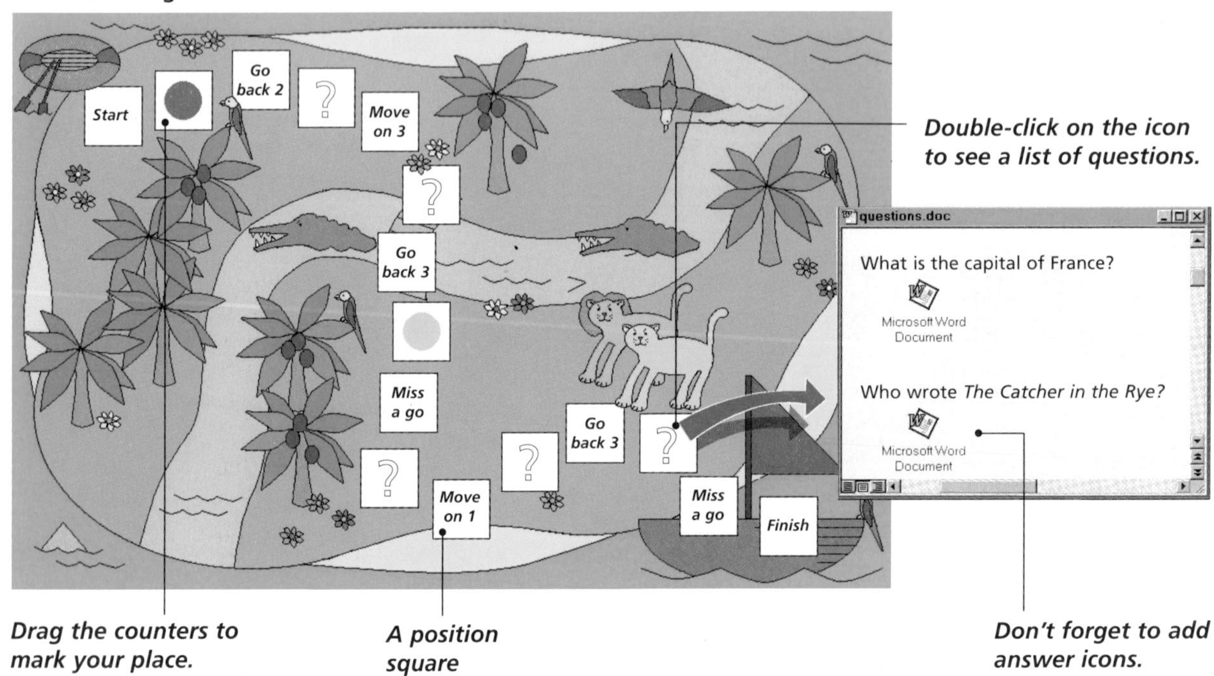

33 BUILD A MYSTERY MANSION

Invent a picture-based mystery and then ask a friend to solve it. As with project 32, you'll need to use an advanced word-processing program, such as *Microsoft® Word*.

First you need to develop an idea to base the mystery on. In this example, a stolen painting is hidden somewhere in a spooky old house. The aim of the game is to find the painting by following clues and descriptions left around the house.

As with project 32, use *Paint* to draw a basic plan or picture of a mystery mansion. Then select and copy it. Create a new document in *Word* and add the picture to it.

You can use *Object Packager* to add the files containing the clues. You could disguise these files as objects in the house. To add an object that overlaps a picture, you need to draw a text box first (see project 32). Click in the text box and follow the technique described in project 30 to package an object. You could insert documents containing descriptions that create atmosphere and suspense.

Don't make the game too easy. In the example below, you would need to open lots of files before you would find the painting. But it's important to leave some clues to help your friend to solve the mystery. To play the game, your friend simply needs to explore the house by double-clicking on pictures to find out about them. The game is over when they discover where the painting is hidden.

The mystery mansion contains lots of files which are disguised as parts of the house.

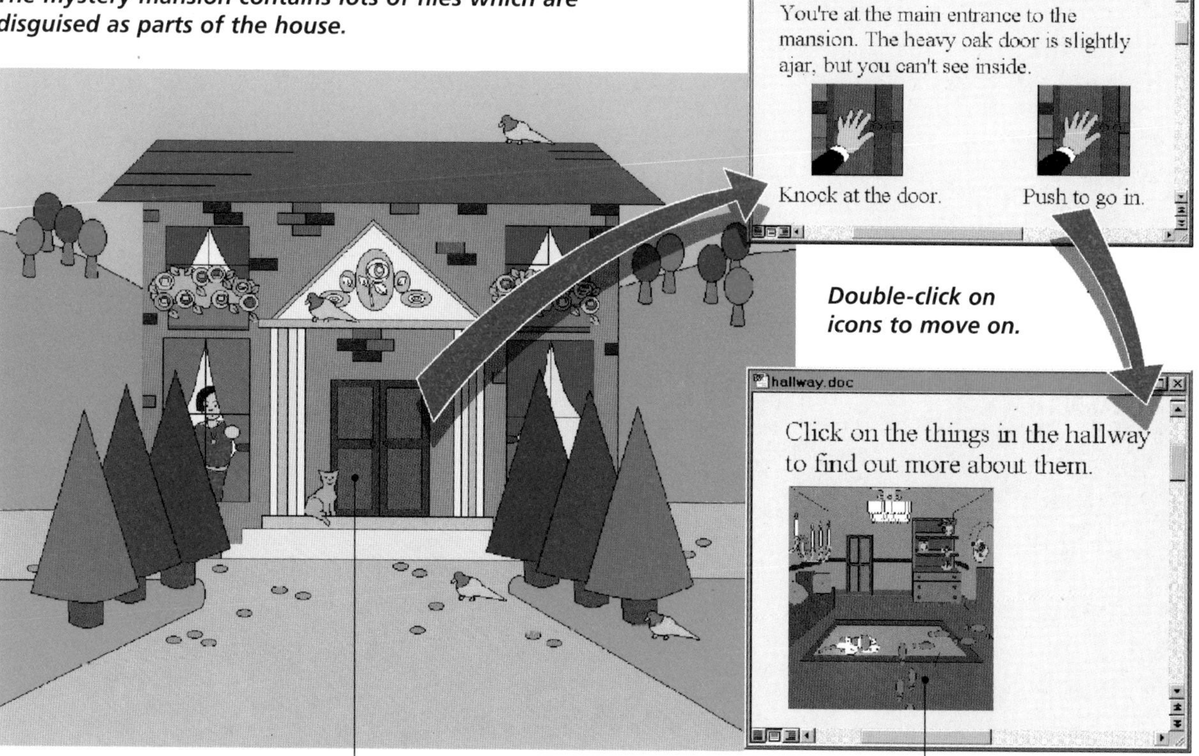

Double-click on icons to move on.

Double-clicking on the door opens a text file.

Don't forget to leave clues, like these muddy footprints.

If you have *Windows® 95*, you can customize your display to give your computer a more personal look. You can transform your pointer into a dinosaur, draw a picture to cover your desktop, or add shortcuts to games or programs that you use often. To do this, you need to open the *Control Panel* from the *Settings* menu on the *Start* menu.

34 WALLPAPER YOUR DESKTOP

You can cover your computer's display, or desktop, with a patterned layer called wallpaper.

To look at wallpaper samples, double-click on the *Display* icon in the *Control Panel* and select the *Background* tab in the *Display Properties* box. *Windows® 95* has several designs to choose from. To view a design on the example screen, click on its name in the *Wallpaper* list.

Click on the *Tile* or *Center* option to indicate where you want your wallpaper to be positioned (see below). Then select the name of the wallpaper you want to use and click on *OK* to put it on your desktop.

The Center option puts one copy of the wallpaper design in the middle of the desktop.

The Tile option covers the entire desktop with wallpaper.

35 DESIGN YOUR OWN WALLPAPER

Try designing your own wallpaper to go on your computer's desktop. You'll need to use a drawing or painting program such as *Windows® 95's Paint*.

Launch *Paint*. Select *Attributes* from the *Image* menu to specify a canvas size. For tiled wallpaper, it's better to use a small canvas. Keep your picture simple, as this will look most effective when it is repeated lots of times. When you have finished, save your design in the *Windows* folder on the C drive.

If you are using *Paint*, select *Set As Wallpaper (Tiled)* from the *File* menu to put your wallpaper on the desktop. Alternatively, follow the procedure in project 34 and select your wallpaper from the *Wallpaper* list. Then click on OK to put it on the desktop.

Ideas for wallpaper

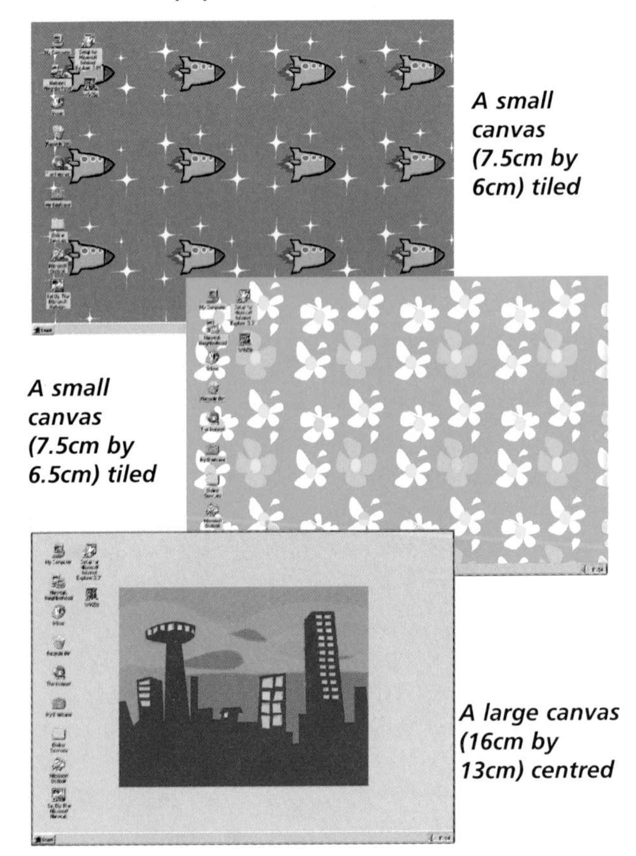

A small canvas (7.5cm by 6cm) tiled

A small canvas (7.5cm by 6.5cm) tiled

A large canvas (16cm by 13cm) centred

36 CHANGE YOUR COLOUR SCHEME

Are you bored with the colours on your display? It's easy to change them to suit your personal taste. Double-click on the *Display* icon in the *Control Panel* and select the *Appearance* tab. An example display will show the colours currently being used on your screen.

To alter the colours, click on the part of the display you want to change, or select its name from the *Item* list. Then choose a colour for that item from the *Color* list.

You can also change the style of text used in *Menu* and *Title* bars. Simply select a style from the *Font* box and use the boxes beside it to change the size and colour of the text.

When you have chosen colours for your display, click on the *Save As* button to save and name your colour scheme. It will then appear on the *Scheme* list with the other *Windows*® *95* colour schemes. Select your scheme and click on *OK* to use it for your display.

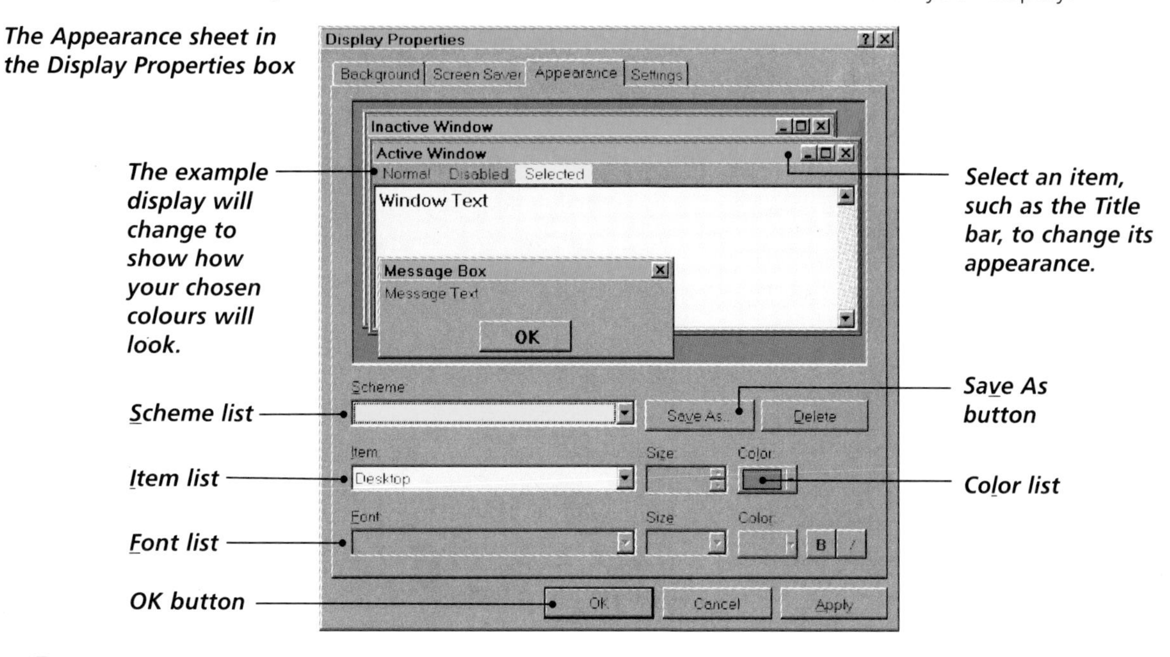

The Appearance sheet in the Display Properties box

37 ADD SHORTCUTS

In *Windows*® *95*, you can put handy shortcuts on your computer's desktop for the programs and documents that you use most often. This shortcut can then be used to open these files quickly and easily.

To add a shortcut for a particular program, first you need to find its name in *Windows*® *Explorer*. Most program files are found in the *Programs* folder within the *Start Menu* folder in the *Windows* folder. If you can't find a program, use the *Find* program on the *Start* menu to search for it.

Make sure you can see your desktop. (You may need to drag some windows out of the way.) Then click on the program's name with the right mouse button and drag its icon onto the desktop. When you release the mouse button a menu will appear. Select *Create Shortcut(s) Here*.

The shortcut will look similar to the program's icon but with a small arrow added. To start a program from its shortcut, simply double-click on the icon.

Shortcut icon

38 SET UP A SCREEN SAVER

With some older computer screens, if the same image is displayed for a long time, the screen can be left with a permanent imprint of that image. Screen savers were invented to protect the screen by replacing the image with a moving picture after a certain period of time. Modern screens don't need this protection, but people still use screen savers to brighten up their computers.

There are all kinds of fun and lively screen savers. A small selection is supplied with *Windows® 95*, but screen saver programs are also available on the Internet and on free disks supplied with some computing magazines. Turn to projects 71 and 88 for advice on finding and copying files from the Internet.

When you find a good screen saver, you can use *Windows® Explorer* to copy it into the *System* folder in the *Windows* folder on your C drive. To set up a screen saver, double-click on the *Display* icon in the *Control Panel* and select the *Screen Saver* tab. Open the drop-down list of screen savers and select one of the names. The example screen will show what the screen saver looks like.

A screen saver starts when you haven't touched your keyboard or mouse for a certain period of time. You can define this time period in the *Wait* box. Then click on *OK*. Your screen saver is now set up.

The Screen Saver property sheet

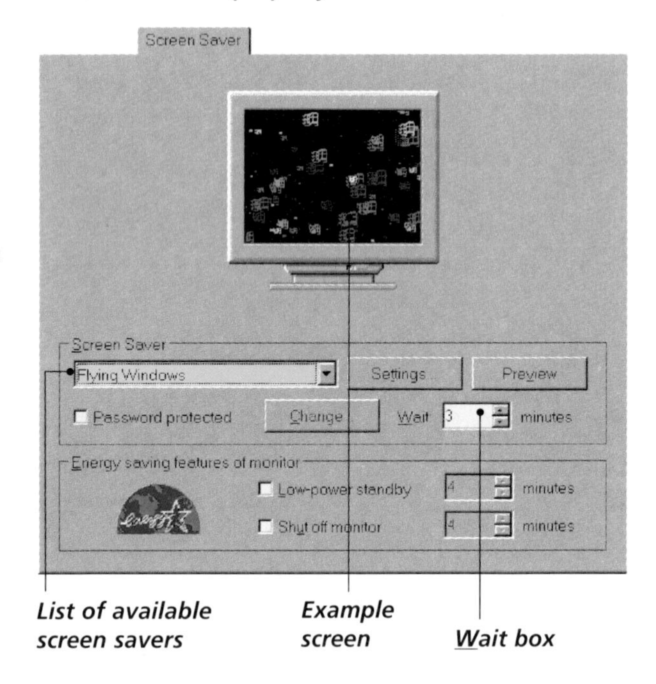

39 WRITE A SCREEN MESSAGE

There are some screen savers that you can personalize. For example, *Windows® 95* has a screen saver called *Scrolling Marquee* which allows you to type in a message. Your message then scrolls across the screen to act as a screen saver.

Follow the instructions in project 38 for setting up a screen saver. Select *Scrolling Marquee* from the drop-down list of screen savers and then click on the *Settings* button. Type your screen message in the *Text* box. You can change the background colour, font size and colour, and the speed at which the text moves across your screen. When you have finished selecting your preferences, click on *OK*.

There are many different kinds of screen saver that you can personalize in this way. Some allow you to add your own picture, which will then move around the screen.

Make a statement with a Scrolling Marquee screen message.

40 ANIMATE YOUR POINTER

If you have *Windows*® *95*, you can change your mouse pointers into animated pictures. As with the screen savers in project 38, you'll need to hunt around for good ones. Turn to projects 71 and 88 for tips on finding and copying things from the Internet. Copy your new pointers, or cursors, into the *Cursors* folder in the *Windows* folder on your C drive.

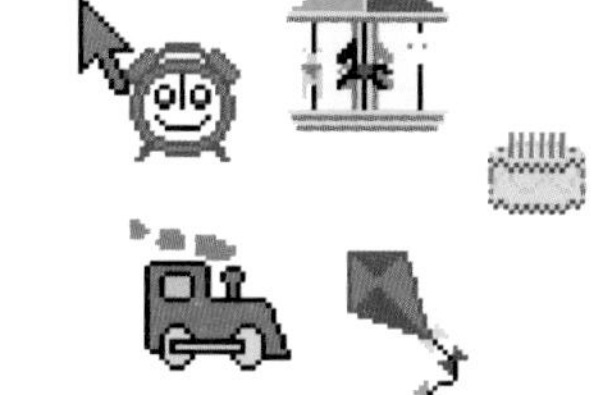

Animated cursors from Internet address http://kwebdesign.com/kdesk/cursor.html

To replace a pointer, double-click on the *Mouse* icon in the *Control Panel* and select the *Pointers* tab. Select the pointer you want to change. Then click on the *Browse* button. The box that opens will show the pointers you copied into the *Cursors* folder. Select the pointer you want to use to replace the existing pointer and click on the *Open* button.

You can change several pointers if you want. When you have finished, click on the *Save As* button to save and name the collection of pointers you have chosen as a group or "scheme". Then click on *OK* to start using them as your new pointers.

The Pointers property sheet

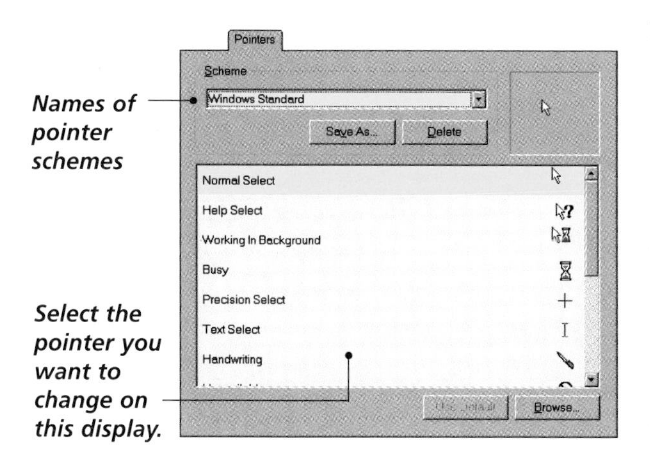

Names of pointer schemes

Select the pointer you want to change on this display.

41 USE A PASSWORD

If you share your computer with other people, it doesn't mean they share your taste in wallpaper and display colours. You can arrange a password system, so that your chosen colours and designs will only appear when you use the computer.

First, make sure all your programs and files are closed. Then double-click on the *Passwords* icon in the *Control Panel,* and select the *User Profiles* tab. Select *Users can customize their preferences...* and make sure that both options in the *User Profile Settings* section are selected. Click on *OK*. A message will appear asking whether you want to restart the computer. Click on *Yes*.

The System Settings Change message box

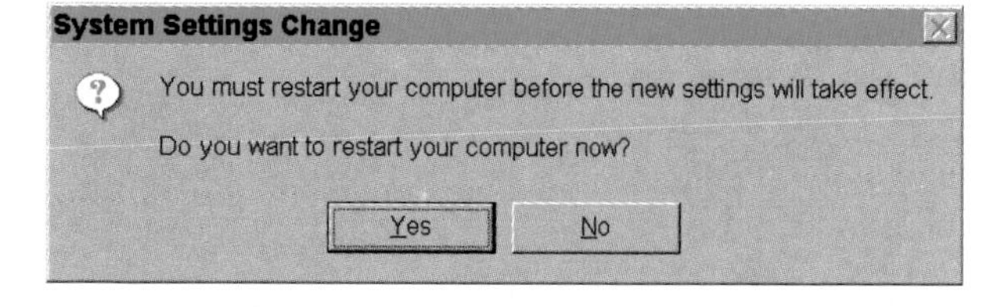

When your computer starts up again, a *Welcome* box will appear. Type your name in the *User name* box and then click in the *Password* box to enter a password. Make sure you choose one that you can easily remember. Click on *OK* when you have typed it.

You will then be asked to type your password again to make sure it is correct. Type it carefully in the *Confirm new password* box and click on *OK*. A message will ask whether you would like to retain your individual settings. Click on *Yes*. The next person who accesses the computer with a different password will be able to change the colours and designs on the display without affecting your personalized settings.

Organize your time efficiently by keeping a computer diary. If you're forgetful, it can give you handy reminders. If you're already well organized, it will help you to plan ahead. There are lots of programs that enable you to keep track of events and appointments. In this section, you will find out how to use a program called *Microsoft® Schedule+*.

42 KEEP A COMPUTER DIARY

A computer diary is very flexible. The information you type can be viewed in several different ways. You can look at a plan of your activities on a particular day, or view the week, month, or year ahead.

To create a diary, or schedule, launch *Schedule+*. Type your name in the *User name* box and click on *OK*. Then select *I want to create a new schedule file* and click on *OK*. In the box that appears, type a name for your schedule in the *File name* box and then click on *Save*. A blank schedule will appear. This will be your personal diary, where you can note down forthcoming events or appointments.

The tabs along the left edge of the window represent the different ways of storing information. If any of the tabs mentioned in this project is not displayed in your window, select *Tab Gallery* from the *View* menu and add the tab to the list.

A Microsoft Schedule+ window

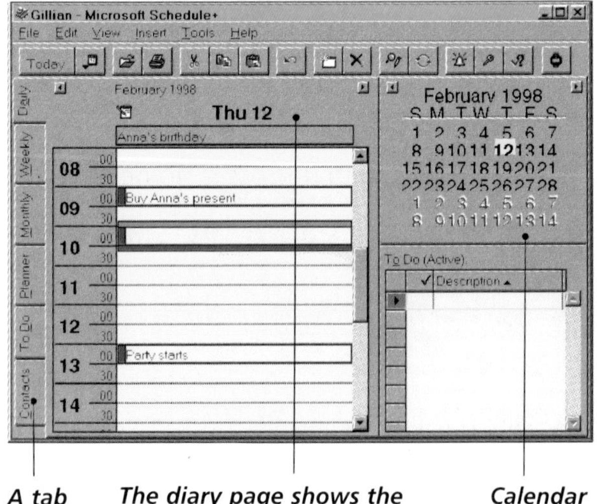

A tab ***The diary page shows the date selected on the calendar.*** ***Calendar***

To add an appointment to your diary, select the *Daily* tab. This shows a plan for a selected day. Select the date of your appointment on the calendar. The diary "page" will change to the date you have selected. Select the time slot where you want to add your appointment and click on *Appointment* on the *Insert* menu. In the box that appears, type in the details of your appointment in the *Description* section, and then click on *OK*. The description will appear in the relevant time slot. It will also appear on the *Weekly*, *Monthly* and *Yearly* sheets.

An Appointment box

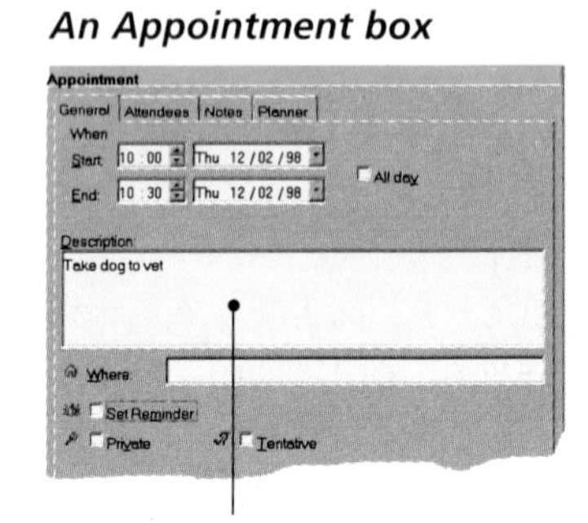

Type a description of the appointment here.

Items that relate to a whole day, or a number of days, rather than a specific time, are called events. To add an event, such as a holiday or birthday, to your diary, you need to select *Event* from the *Insert* menu. For an event lasting several days, such as a holiday, you need to specify the dates the event covers. On the *Daily* and *Weekly* tabs, these events will appear above the main schedule. On the *Monthly* tab, they will be included on each day that they relate to.

To change a diary entry, you need to select it and then select *Edit Item* from the *Edit* menu. You can delete an entry by selecting it and then clicking on the *Delete* button. Don't forget to save any changes you make.

43 SET A REMINDER

You can use *Schedule+* to jog your memory about forthcoming events. For example, you could set a reminder that will appear a few days before someone's birthday, so that you have time to send a card. Or, if you're busy playing a computer game, but don't want to be late for school, set a reminder for half an hour before school is due to start. A reminder box will then appear at the time that you have specified.

A reminder box

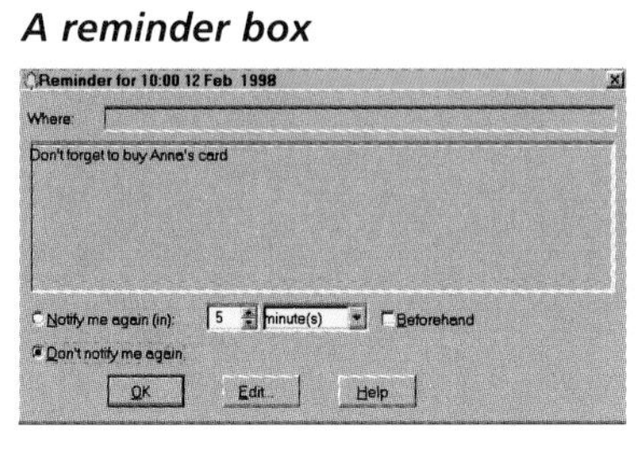

Launch *Schedule+* and type in your name to open your diary (see project 42). Click on the event for which you would like to set a reminder and select *Edit Item* from the *Edit* menu. In the box that appears, select the *General* tab. Select *Set Reminder*. In the box beside it, indicate how long before the event you want to be reminded and then click on *OK*.

Select *Options* from the *Tools* menu. Click on the *General* tab and make sure *Enable reminders* is selected. If an event is just about to happen, leave your computer on and the *Schedule+* program open, to make sure you get the reminder on time. Minimize the program's window to clear it out of the way, so that you can work with other programs. Then, when the time comes, a reminder box will appear on your screen. If you switch your computer off, but leave *Schedule+* open, your reminder will appear next time you switch on.

44 MAKE A LIST OF THINGS TO DO

You can make a *To Do* list to help you organize all the important things you have to do. For example, you could use it to help you plan your homework timetable.

Launch *Schedule+* and type in your name to open your diary (see project 42). Select the *To Do* tab. A grid will be displayed. Select *Columns* from the *View* menu and then choose *Few*.

Click in an empty box in the *Description* column, and type in a description of a homework assignment. In the *Priority* section, indicate how important the assignment is by typing in a number between 1 and 9. (1 is the most important and 9 is the least important.)

Click in the *Ends* column to indicate the date by which the homework needs to be completed. Open the drop-down list and select the date on the calendar.

Your homework assignments will automatically be listed in order of priority. When you have completed an assignment, click on the box in front of the task description to cross that task off your list. If you click on a task by mistake, click again to uncross it. To delete a task completely, click on it and press the delete key on your keyboard. You can change the order of the assignments by using the *Sort* and *Filter* commands on the *View* menu.

You can use a To Do List to organize important tasks.

	✓	Description ▲	Priority ▲	Ends ▲
		⊟ Project: (None)		
		Geography project	1	Sun 01/03/98
		French translation	2	Fri 20/02/98
▶	✓	~~Literature assignment~~	~~3~~	~~Tue 03/02/98~~
*				

You can set up an address book or catalogue your music collection using a database program. This allows you to store information which you can then organize in lots of different ways. The instructions in this section show how to make simple databases using a database program called *Microsoft® Access*. Other similar programs you could use include *Paradox, Approach* and *FoxPro*. Some of the later projects in this section use information from the earlier ones, so you'll need to read through all the projects in order.

45 SET UP AN ADDRESS BOOK

Use a database to store your friends' addresses. Launch *Access*. Select *Database Wizard* and click on *OK*. Then click on the *Databases* tab. Select the *Address Book.mdz* icon and click on *OK*. In the dialog box that opens, type a name for your database file in the *File name* box. Then click on *Create*.

After a few seconds, the *Database Wizard* will start. The first screen tells you what kind of information the database will include. Click on *Next*. On the second screen, you'll see a list of categories, called fields, such as address and telephone number. Select the fields that you want to include in your database and then click on *Next*. On the following screens, you can choose styles for screen displays and for documents to be printed, called reports. When you have selected the styles you want, click on *Next* to continue. Type the title you want to use in the database window and click on *Finish*.

Choose between different screen styles.

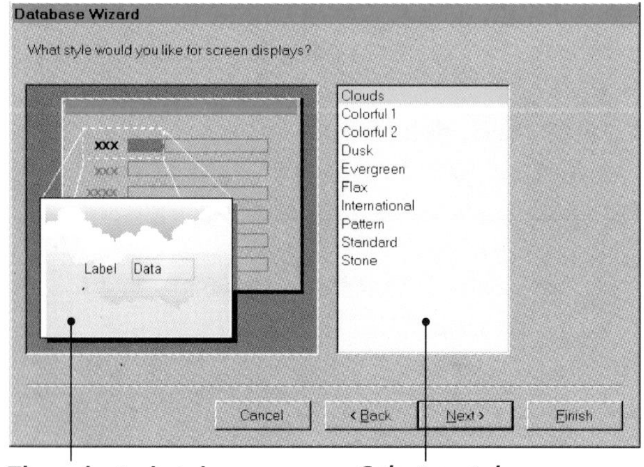

The selected style is displayed here.

Select a style from this list.

It takes the computer a short time to create the database. When it has finished, click on the *Enter/View Addresses* button on the *Main Switchboard*. An on-screen form containing the fields you selected will appear. Type in the details of one of your friends, using the Tab key on your keyboard to move between fields. A set of details for one person is called a record. To add another record, click on the *New Record* button (see below). When you have finished adding records, close the *Form* window.

Main switchboard

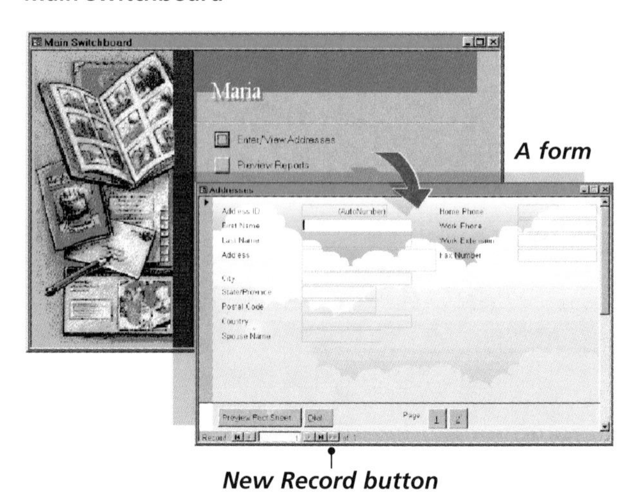

A form

New Record button

The *Address Book Wizard* organizes the information you typed in a number of ways, such as in order of surname or according to birthdays. This is then displayed in neat reports. To see a list of the different reports, click on the *Preview Reports* button on the *Main Switchboard*. Then click on a button to see a preview of a report.

46 MAKE AN INVITATION LIST

You can use the information in a database in lots of useful ways. For example, if you were giving a party, and wanted to invite friends living in your town or city, you could use your address book to make a guest list.

To do this, you need to create a "query". A query searches for information that fits certain criteria - in this case, friends who live in the same city as you. Open the *Address Book* database you created in project 45. To do this, launch *Access*. In the box that appears, select *Open an Existing Database* and click on *OK*. Select your database and click on *Open*. Maximize the minimized window in the bottom left corner. A window like the one below will appear.

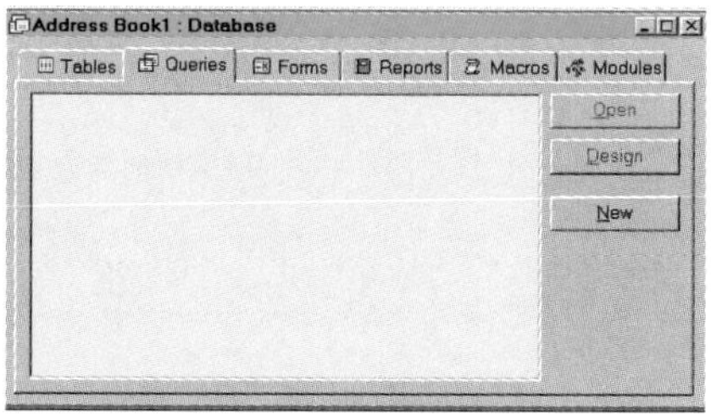

Address Book: Database window

Address Book1 : Database
Tables | Queries | Forms | Reports | Macros | Modules
Open
Design
New

Select the *Queries* tab and click on *New*. Select *Simple Query Wizard* and click on *OK*. Open the *Table/Queries* list and select *Table: Addresses*. A list of fields will appear in the *Available Fields* box. Double-click on a field to include it in your query. For this one, add *FirstName, LastName, Address, City, PostalCode*. Then click on *Next*.

Make sure *Modify the query design* is selected. Name your query **Invitation Query** and click on *Finish*.

A grid will appear. In the *Criteria* section of the *City* field, type the name of your city in quotation marks. Select *Save As* from the *File* menu and save your query. Then click on the *Run* button on the *Toolbar* in the main window. Your invitation list will be displayed. To print it out, select *Print* from the *File* menu.

Part of the Query Design grid

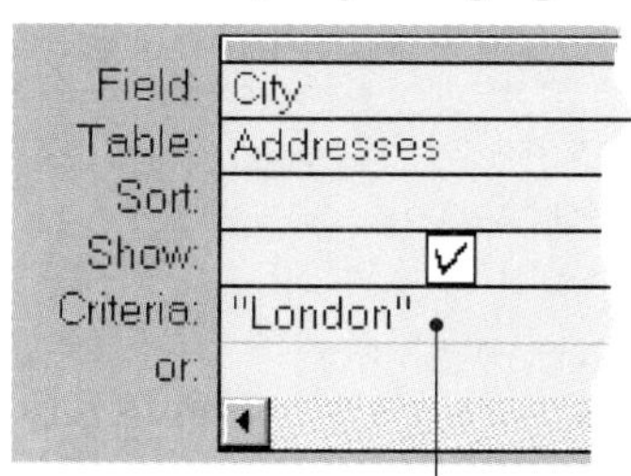

Type your city's name here.

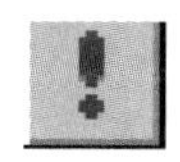

Run button

47 PRINT ADDRESS LABELS

Use the information from the query you made in project 46 to print out address labels for your invitations. Make sure you buy labels that are suitable to use with your printer.

Launch *Access*, and open your *Address Book* database (see project 45). Select the *Reports* tab and click on *New*. Select *Label Wizard*. Open the drop-down list and click on Invitation Query. Then click on *OK*. On the first screen, select the size of labels you are using and click on *Next*. Choose a font for the text on your label. Click on *Next*. Arrange the label layout as shown on the right. To add a field, double-click on its name. Leave a space between each field, and press Return to start a new line. When you have finished, click on *Next*.

Click on *Next* to move on again. Name your report and select *See the labels as they will look printed*. Click on *Finish*. A preview of the address labels will appear. Load the label sheets into your printer and select *Print* from the *File* menu.

Label layout

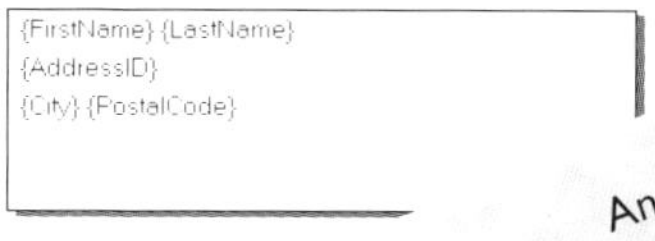

{FirstName} {LastName}
{AddressID}
{City} {PostalCode}

Printed labels

Anna Hadley
42 High Street
London W2 6HL

48 CATALOGUE YOUR MUSIC COLLECTION

Use a database to organize your CDs and tapes so that you know exactly what you've got in your music collection.

Launch *Access,* select *Database Wizard* and click on *OK.* Click on the *Databases* tab. Select the *Music Collection.mdz* icon and click on *OK.* Type a name for your new database in the *File name* box and click on *Create.* After a few seconds, the *Music Collection Wizard* will start. Read the information on each screen, clicking on the *Next* button when you want to move to the next screen.

In the *Music Collection* database, there are separate tables for storing information about the recording artist, the recording itself, and the individual tracks. You can include field names from each of these tables in your database, as shown in the example below. When you have given all the information the *Wizard* requires, click on the *Finish* button to create the database.

A Music Collection Database Wizard screen

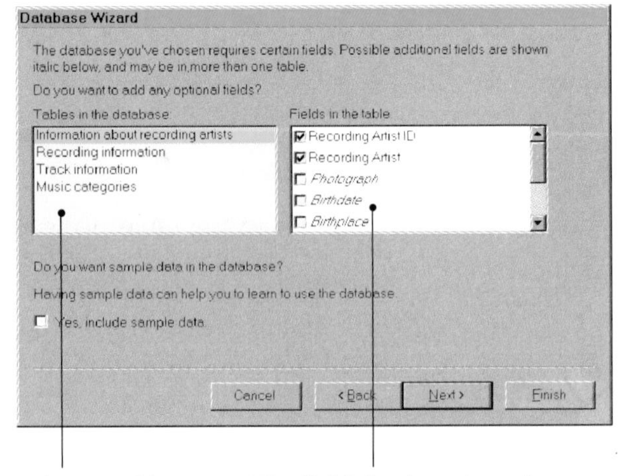

Select a table from this list.

The fields in the selected table will be displayed here.

When the computer has finished creating the database, click on *Enter/View Recordings* on the *Main Switchboard.* An on-screen form like the one below will appear. Type in the details of your music collection.

You'll notice that some of the fields, for example *Recording Artist,* have a drop-down list button on the right-hand side. This is because these fields are included in more than one table. To add an artist's details, double-click in the *Recording Artist* box. A second form representing the *Recording Artist* table will appear. When you have filled in the details on this form, close its window. If you have a second recording by the same artist, you won't need to type in the details again. Simply open the drop-down list and select the artist's name.

A Recordings form

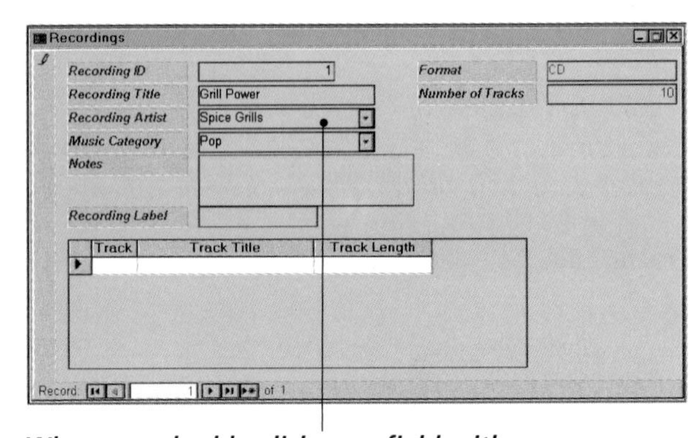

When you double-click on a field with an arrow beside it, another form will open.

You should save the information you type at regular intervals. To do this, select *Save As* from the *File* menu in the main window and save and name your database. Once you have named the database, use the *Save* command to save the details now and again. Then look at projects 49 and 50 to find out what you can do with all the information you have stored.

49 SEARCH FOR A SONG

You can list the recordings in your *Music Collection* database (see project 48) in different ways. For example, you could list them by the bands that made them or the year they were recorded. You could even search for songs with a particular word in the title. For instance, for a Christmas party, you could search for titles containing the word Christmas.

Launch *Access* and open your *Music Collection* database. Maximize the minimized window in the bottom left corner. In the *Music Collection: Database* window, select the *Queries* tab and click on *New*. Then select *Simple Query Wizard* and click on *OK*.

To select the fields to be included in your query, open the *Tables/Queries* drop-down list and select *Table:Tracks*.

Double-click on *TrackTitle* on the *Available Fields* list to add it to the *Selected Fields* list. Open the drop-down list again and select *Table:Recordings*. Double-click on *RecordingTitle* and then *RecordingArtistID* on the *Available Fields* list. Click on *Next*. On the next screen, make sure *Modify the query design* is selected. Name the query **Song Title query** and click on *Finish*.

In the grid that appears, click in the *Criteria* section of the *Track/Title* field. Type **Like "*Christmas*"**. This tells the program to search for titles containing the word in quotation marks. Click on the *Run* button (see project 46) to see a list of songs that fit this description. Select *Save As* from the *File* menu and save your query.

50 CUSTOMIZE A DATABASE

Add an extra field to your *Music Collection* database to note where your recordings are, whether they're in a shoe box under your bed or you've lent them to a friend.

Launch *Access* and open your *Music Collection* database (see project 48). Maximize the minimized window and select the *Tables* tab. Then select the *Recordings* icon and click on *Design*. A list of the fields in the *Recordings* table will appear. To add an extra field, click in an empty box in the *Field Name* list and type **Location**. Click in the box beside it (on the *Data Type* list) and select *Text* from the drop-down list. This indicates that the information to be typed into this field is text, rather than, for example, a date or a number. Select *Save* from the *File* menu to save the changes to the table. To type in the location details of each recording, select *Datasheet* from the *View* menu. Use the scroll bar to move to the field headed *Location*. Click on each line to type in the location of that recording. Then select *Save Layout* from the *File* menu. Now, as long as you remember to update your database, you'll always be able to find your recordings.

The Recordings: Table window

Recordings : Table

Field Name	Data Type
MusicCategoryID	Number
NumberofTracks	Number
Location	Text

Text
Memo
Number
Date/Time
Currency
AutoNumber
Yes/No
OLE Object
Lookup Wizard

You can use tables called spreadsheets to help you make calculations. In this section, you'll find out how to use a spreadsheet program called *Microsoft® Excel*. Spreadsheets can be used to store and organize all kinds of numerical information. For example, you can use a spreadsheet to work out what you spend your money on, and to produce graphs to display this information.

51 CHART YOUR SPENDING MONEY

You can use a spreadsheet to keep a record of how you spend your money.

To do this, launch *Excel*. You'll see a blank table made up of rows and columns. The individual boxes in the table are called cells. Click in the first cell in the first column. This is cell A1. Type **Spent On**. Use this column to list the things that you spend money on. Click in cell B1 and type **Amount**. In this column, note the amount of money that you spend on each of the items in column A. If you run out of space, you can widen a column by clicking on the edge of the label at the top of the column and dragging it.

Use this example spreadsheet to help you to type in details of how you spend your money.

A column heading

Book1

	A	B	C	D
1	Spent On	Amount		
2	Films	12		
3	CDs	12.99		
4	Magazines	3.55		
5	Books	15.5		
6				
7				

Sheet1 / Sheet2 / She

A row

Click and drag here to widen a column.

Each box is called a cell.

When you have finished typing in the information, click on column heading B. Select *Cells* on the *Format* menu. Click on the *Number* tab. Select *Currency* from the *Category* list and click on *OK*. This tells the computer that you will be typing in money values.

To represent the information you have typed as a pie chart, first you need to select it. Click in cell A2 and drag across and down to highlight all the information except the column titles. Click on the *ChartWizard* button on the *Standard* toolbar. Move the cursor to a blank area of the spreadsheet and click and drag to create a box for the pie chart.

ChartWizard button

In the *ChartWizard* box that appears, click on *Next*. Select *3-D Pie* from the chart options and click on *Next*. Choose option number 7 to create a pie chart like the one below. Click on *Next*. For *Data Series*, select the *Columns* option. Enter the value **1** for *Use First _ Column(s) for Pie Slice Labels*. Type **0** for *Use First _ Row(s) for Chart Title*. Click on *Next*. In answer to the question *Add a Legend?*, click on *No*. Finally, type a title for your chart and click on *Finish*. A chart like the one below will appear. Select *Save As* from the *File* menu to save and name your spreadsheet.

A spending money pie chart

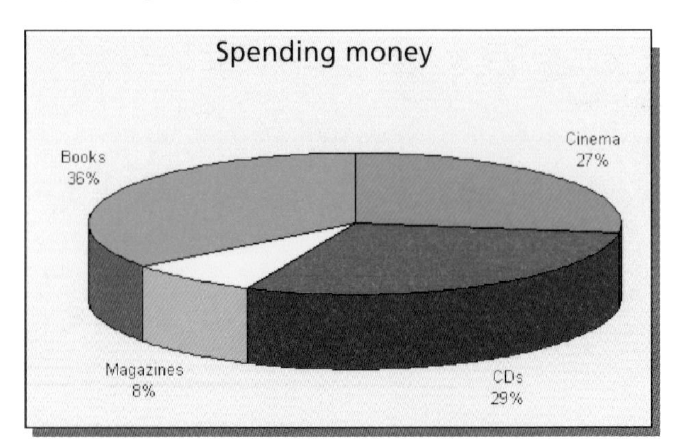

52 ADD UP TOTALS

Use a spreadsheet to calculate how much money you have, with the amounts you type automatically being added or subtracted.

Launch *Excel*. Click in cell A1 and type **Date**. Then type **Amount** in B1, **Description** in C1 and **Running total** in D1. Make the columns wider if you need to. Beginning on row 3, type in details of money you spend or receive in columns A, B and C. Put a minus sign in front of an amount to indicate money spent. To put the entries in order of date, select the information in the first three columns. Select *Sort* from the *Data* menu. Click on *Column A* on the *Sort By* drop-down list. Select *Ascending* and click on *OK*. Select column B and change the format to currency (see project 51).

Column D will be used to calculate how much money you have left. Click in D3. Type **=D2+B3** and press Return. (This tells the program which amounts to add together.) The cell will now show the same amount as B3. Select D3 again and choose *Copy* from the *Edit* menu. A dotted line will appear around it. Click in the middle of the cell and highlight the cells in column D with entries beside them. Select *Paste* from the *Edit* menu. The running total column will now automatically calculate how much you have after each entry.

A spreadsheet showing running totals

Book1

	A	B	C	D
1	Date	Amount	Description	Running total
2				
3	22/02/98	10.00	Pocket money	10.00
4	24/02/98	-5.00	Cinema	5.00
5	26/02/98	-3.99	Book	1.01
6	29/02/98	15.00	Birthday money	16.01

Sheet1 / Sheet2 / Sheet3 / She

This column shows how much money you have.

53 MAKE PREDICTIONS

You can use spreadsheets to help you to plan the best way of spending your money. Launch *Excel* and open the spreadsheet you created in project 52. You can add items that you would like to buy to the list of things you have already bought. You can then see how this will affect your finances. Select cell D3 and click on *Copy* on the *Edit* menu. Click and drag to highlight all the cells that have entries beside them. Select *Paste* from the *Edit* menu. Totals for all your new entries will appear.

Using the *Chart Wizard* (see project 51), see whether you can display your predictions in a column graph like the one below. You'll need to select the information in columns C and D.

When the bars in your column graph appear below the 0.00 line, it means you don't have enough money.

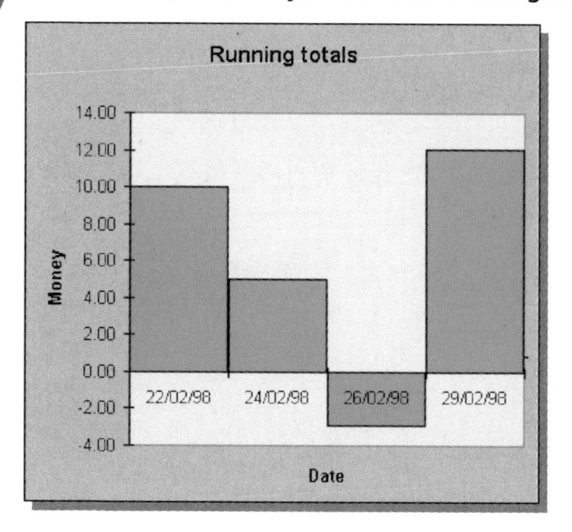

Change some of the values in the Amount column to see how buying certain things would affect your finances. For example, if you buy a CD this week, will you still have enough money to go to the cinema? The Totals column and the graph will change to show what will happen if you spent your money in that way.

This section involves working with sound and animation. You'll need special equipment to carry out most of these projects. Find out what you need on page 61.

54 PLAY A MUSIC CD

If your computer has a CD-ROM drive, you can use it to play music CDs. *Windows® 95* has a program called *CD Player* to help you do this. (For this project, your speakers or headphones need to be plugged into the appropriate socket on your computer.)

Launch *CD Player* by clicking on its name. It's usually found in the *Multimedia* folder in the *Accessories* program group. Then simply insert a music CD and click on the *Play* button to start it playing.

Part of the CD Player window

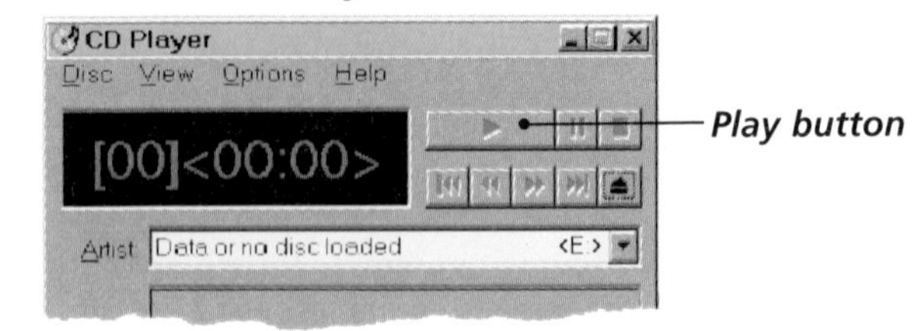

55 ARRANGE A PLAY LIST

You can use *CD Player* to arrange a "play list". This means that the tracks on a CD will be played in the order that you select.

First you need to enter information about your CD. Place the CD in the CD-ROM drive. Launch *CD Player* and select *Edit Play List* from the *Disc* menu. Type the artist's name in the *Artist* box and the CD's title in the *Title* box. The tracks are listed by number. To enter their names, click on a track number in the *Available Tracks* box and type its title in the *Track* box. Click on *Set Name* to confirm the details.

Click on *Clear All* to create a blank play list. Then, in the *Available Tracks* box, select the name of a track you want to add to it and click on *Add*. Repeat this to add more tracks. When you have finished, click on *OK*. Click on the *Play* button to play the tracks on your list. Next time you use this CD, your computer will recognize it, and display the details you have entered.

CD Player: Disc Settings box

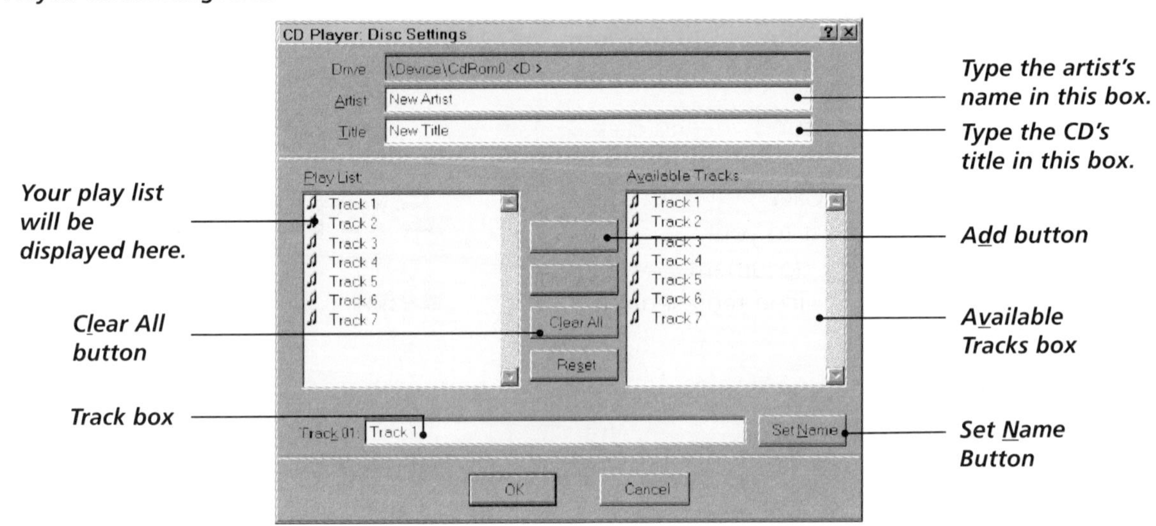

56 RECORD A SOUND

It's easy to record sounds using *Windows® 95's Sound Recorder* program. Try making a short voice recording.

Attach a microphone to your computer (see pages 60 to 62) and make sure it is switched on. Launch *Sound Recorder* (from the *Multimedia* folder in the *Accessories* program group). Click on the *Record* button to start recording. Then speak into the microphone. When you have finished, click on the *Stop* button.

You have now recorded a sound file. To save and name it, select *Save As* from the *File* menu. At the bottom of the *Save As* box, you are told the size of the file. Sound files can take up lots of space on your hard disk. You can make a file smaller by saving it at lower quality. This means that when you play it back it won't sound quite as clear. To do this, click on the *Change* button and select a smaller file size (less than 172 KB/s) from the *Attributes* list. Once you have saved your sound file, click on the *Play* button in *Sound Recorder* to hear it.

A Sound Recorder window

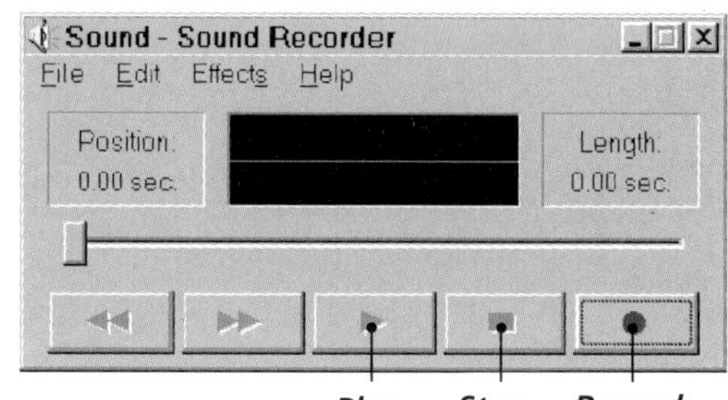

57 SEND A MULTIMEDIA GREETING

You can insert sound files into documents. Try adding a short voice message to a birthday greeting or letter. First, follow the instructions in project 56 to record and save your sound file. You could record a personal message or even sing Happy Birthday.

Open the document that you want to add your sound file to, and place the cursor where you want it to appear. Select *Object* from the *Insert* menu. Then select the *Create From File* option and click on *Browse*. Find and select your sound file and click on the *Insert* button. Click on *OK* to add it to your document. An icon representing the sound file will appear in your document. Double-click on it to hear the sound file.

To send your greeting to a friend, save it onto a floppy disk. To play the message, your friend will need to have a computer with a sound card and similar software to yours.

A multimedia greetings message

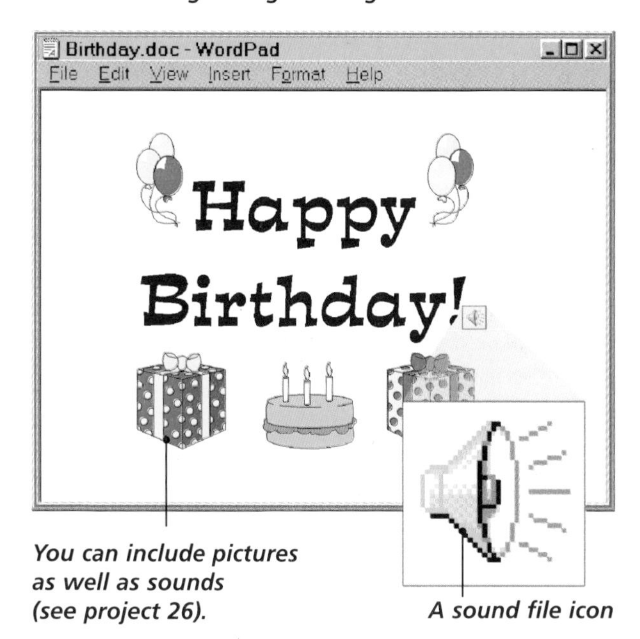

You can include pictures as well as sounds (see project 26).

A sound file icon

58 INVENT A MUSIC QUIZ

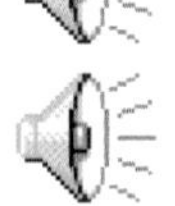

Use your word-processing skills to lay out the quiz document neatly (see project 23).

Add sound files to a quiz document to produce a sound-based music quiz. The quiz involves listening to a piece of music and then answering questions about it. Find the music you want to use on a CD or tape (or you could hum the tunes yourself). Use *Sound Recorder* to record each piece of music as a separate sound file (see project 56). Then, you need to think of a question to ask about each recording (see the examples above).

Use a word-processing program such as *WordPad* to create a text document. Type in your quiz and then insert each sound file beside the relevant question, using the technique described in project 57. To play the game, all a "contestant" needs to do is read the question and then double-click on a sound icon to hear the recording. The hard part is trying to guess the answers.

Be careful. Recording sounds can take up lots of space in your computer's memory, so you should only use short sections of music.

59 EDIT A SOUND

Once you have recorded a sound, you can cut bits out and change the sound file. This is called editing. There are lots of advanced programs that allow you to do this, but you can try out simple editing with *Windows® 95's Sound Recorder*.

Editing sounds with Sound Recorder

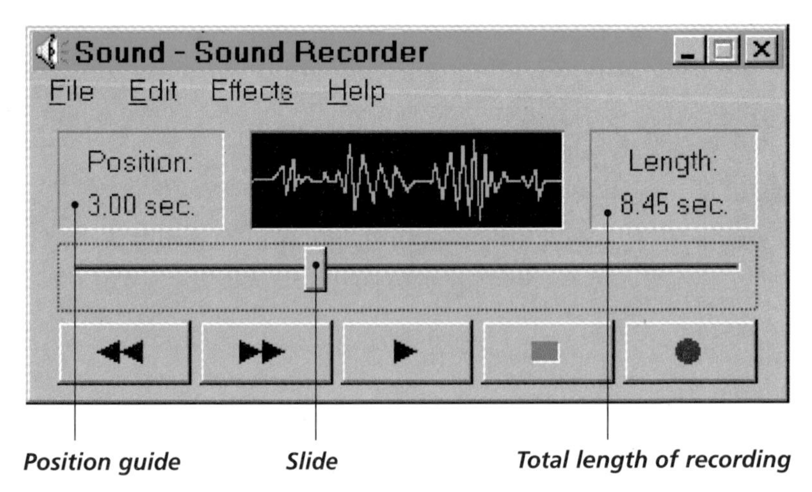

When you make a recording, you may end up with noises that you don't want at the beginning or end. It's easy to tidy up your recording by deleting these.

Launch *Sound Recorder* and open the sound file you want to edit. When you play it, the green line on the display will show the sound's pattern. When you get to the point you want to cut, note the time shown on the position guide. Drag the slide to that point and click on the *Play* button to check that it's the right place. If it is, move the slide back to that point and select *Delete Before Current Position* or *Delete After Current Position* from the *Edit* menu. In the box that appears, click on *OK* to delete the section indicated.

60 ADD SPECIAL EFFECTS

Even with a simple program like *Sound Recorder*, it is possible to add special effects to a recording. Use the commands on the *Effects* menu to add echo, change the speed of a sound, or play it backwards.

These techniques are particularly effective in changing voice recordings. Try it with your friends' voices. Turn high pitched voices into deep booming voices by decreasing speed and adding echo, or increase the speed to make even the deepest voice sound like a cartoon mouse.

61 INVENT A SOUND PUZZLE

Use the techniques described in projects 56 and 57 to record a sound puzzle. Try out your recording skills by recording lots of strange sounds and asking someone to guess what they are.

You could record the sound of a door opening or someone stirring a cup of coffee. Unwanted noises at the beginning or end of the recording could give away the answer. To avoid this, edit the sound, using the method described in project 59 to remove the section you don't want.

62 ASSIGN SOUNDS TO EVENTS

One of the ways that you can customize your computer is by instructing it to play sounds when performing certain actions, for example when closing a program's window or opening a menu.

To do this, you use the *Control Panel*, as in projects 34 to 41. Open the *Control Panel* and double-click on the *Sounds* icon to open the *Sounds Properties* dialog box. The *Events* box contains a list of the different actions, called events, for which you can make a sound play. Select an event. Select the name of a sound from the *Name* drop-down list, or you could use a sound you have recorded yourself. Click on the *Browse* button to search for one of your own sound files.

To hear a preview of a sound, select its name and then click on the *Play* button beside the *Preview* box. When you have found the sound you want to use, select it and click on *OK*. This sound will now play for the event you have selected.

Try to think of suitable sounds to use for different events. For example, you could have a voice message to say hello when *Windows*® *95* starts up.

The Sounds Properties dialog box

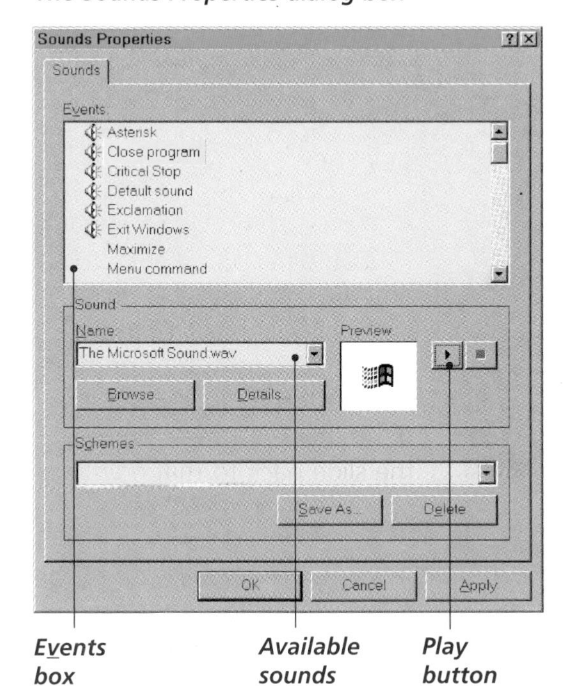

63 MIX SOUNDS

You can use music editing programs to mix different sounds together to produce "fake" recordings, unusual effects, or to spice up a recording by adding extra bits to it. You can do this at a very simple level using the *Sound Recorder* program supplied with *Windows® 95*.

First you need to record some sounds to use. Turn to project 56 to find out how to do this.

There are two different ways that you can combine sounds in *Sound Recorder*. You can insert one sound file into another, or you can "overlay" them so that you hear more than one sound at the same time.

You can use these techniques to change recordings in interesting ways. For example, by piecing together words or phrases from different recordings of your friends' voices, you could make them say something that they didn't actually say.

To insert a sound file, launch *Sound Recorder*. Open the sound file that you want to add a second file to. Play the sound and use the time shown on the position guide to note where you want to insert the sound file. Drag the slide to that position. Select *Insert File* from the *Edit* menu. Find and select the name of the file you want to insert and click on *Open*. The new sound will replace the old sound after the point that you have selected. Go to the beginning of the recording and click on the *Play* button to listen to the entire sound file.

To combine sounds, so that they play at the same time, open the sound file that you want to mix a file with. As above, drag the slide to the place where you want it to appear. Select *Mix With File* from the *Edit* menu. Select the name of the file you want to mix and click on *Open*. The sounds will then be merged together from the point you have selected.

64 DRAW TALKING PICTURES

Projects 28 to 33 describe how to create hidden files. You can use the same technique with sound files. Make a fun, interactive farmyard, with pictures of animals that make the appropriate noises when you double-click on them.

Record your sounds using the technique described in project 56. Then launch *Paint* and draw a picture to use for one of the sounds. When you have finished, select the picture using the *Selection* tool and click on *Copy* on the *Edit* menu.

Launch *WordPad* and create a new document. Using the technique described in project 30, launch *Object Packager*. Paste your picture into the *Appearance* section. Then select the *Content* section and click on *Import* on the *File* menu. Find and select the name of the appropriate sound file and click on *Open*. Select *Update* from the *File* menu and then close the *Object Packager* window.

Your picture will appear in the *WordPad* document. Now, every time you double-click on the picture, your chosen sound will play.

65 MAKE MUSIC

There are lots of different ways to use your computer to make music. There are specialist programs, such as *SimTunes* made by *Maxis*, which allow you to explore and compose music directly from your computer. With *SimTunes,* you do this by creating musical pictures like the one below. You compose a piece of music by instructing the musical bugs to move around the screen in certain ways.

SimTunes offers a creative approach to making music. You can download a demonstration copy (see project 88) from http://www.maxis.com.

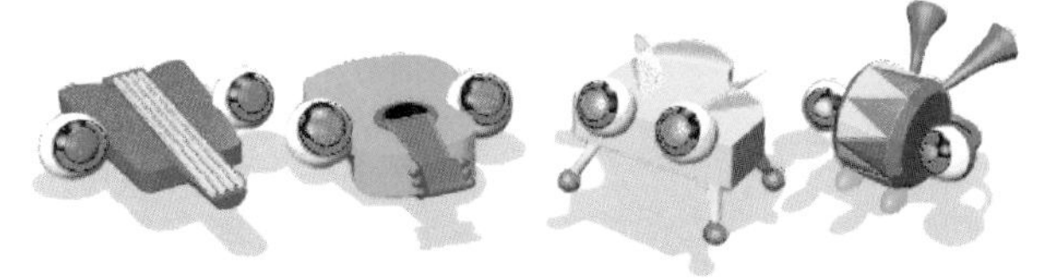

The bugs, shown above, make music as they move around the screen.

There are lots of other types of music programs. Some are like games, but others teach more formal musical skills. For example, there are piano lesson programs and programs that will teach you how to read musical notes.

If you want to get involved in music at an advanced level, you can use your computer to do amazing things. A method of communication called MIDI (Musical Instrument Digital Interface) enables you to link electronic musical instruments, such as keyboards, to your computer. This means that you can play musical notes on your keyboard which will then be transmitted directly to your computer.

Using a program called a sequencer, you can then turn your computer into a mini recording studio. You can compose a piece of music, using your keyboard to record the different instrumental parts one at a time. The sequencer then enables you to put the parts together and play them back at the same time. You can edit the music, rearranging it, making it louder or softer, or adding special effects.

You can use a MIDI keyboard like this one to transmit information directly to your computer.

66 PRESENT A SLIDE SHOW

Use a program called *Microsoft® PowerPoint* (available with the *Microsoft® Office* program package) to arrange an on-screen slide show to present your computer artwork (see projects 1 to 20). You can then flick through your pictures on your computer screen.

Launch *PowerPoint,* select the *Blank Presentation* option and click on *OK*. Select the blank slide option in the *New Slide* box and click on *OK*. A blank slide will appear. To add one of your *Paint* pictures to it, select *Picture* from the *Insert* menu. Find and select the name of the picture you want to add and click on *OK*. The picture will appear on the slide.

Select *New Slide* from the *Insert* menu and repeat this method to add more pictures.

When you have finished, select *Slide Show* on the *View* menu. Select the *All* option in the *Slides* section and select *Manual Advance.* Then click on the *Show* button to start the show. The dialog box and window will disappear and your first slide will be displayed. To move on to the next slide, click anywhere with your left mouse button or press any key on your keyboard.

67 ANIMATE YOUR PICTURES

Specialist animation programs are often expensive. But you can achieve similar results using software that you may already have on your computer. For example, you can set up a simple animation using *PowerPoint.*

Animations are made from sequences of still pictures. Each picture is slightly different from the previous one. When the pictures are displayed one after the other, very quickly, it looks as though a single picture is moving.

Use *Paint* to draw a sequence of pictures like the ones on the right. Save the first picture with the name **frame1.bmp**. Then alter the picture slightly and save it with the name **frame2.bmp**. Use this technique to draw several frames which follow on from one another.

When played back, this series of slides will show the man diving into the water.

Launch *PowerPoint* and select a blank presentation and blank slide (see project 66). Select *Picture* from the *Insert* menu. Find and select frame1.bmp and click on *OK*. Create a slide for each frame in this way.

To arrange the slide display, select *Slide Sorter* from the *View* menu. Click on each slide in turn and select *Slide Transition* from the *Tools* menu. In the *Advance* box, select *Automatically after ... seconds.* Type the value **1** in the seconds box. This will leave a one-second gap between each slide. When you have set this value for each slide, click on *Slide Show* on the *View* menu. Select *All* in the *Slides* section and select *Use Slide Timings.* Click on *Show* to start the animation. The pictures will appear at one-second intervals.

68 BUILD AN UNDERSEA SCENE

Use *PowerPoint* to build a scene made from lots of images. For example, you could arrange an undersea scene which gradually becomes crowded with fish.

First, draw the background scene. In *Paint,* create a canvas 25.4cm wide and 19.5cm high (see project 9). Use the *Fill* tool to shade the canvas blue. Add a few underwater plants at the bottom. You'll need to scroll down the canvas to do this. Save this file with the name **scene.bmp**. On a new canvas (about 6cm wide and 4cm high), draw a picture of a fish. Shade the background surrounding it the same shade of blue as in scene.bmp. Save it and name the file **fish1.bmp**. Draw a selection of sea creatures, each in a separate file.

Launch *PowerPoint* and select a blank presentation and slide (see project 66). Then select *Picture* from the *Insert* menu. Find and select scene.bmp and click on *OK.* The background scene will appear on the slide.

Add the other picture files to the slide in the same way. Drag each one into the position you want, making sure that the blocks containing the fish don't overlap one another.

To arrange animation effects, click on a fish with the right mouse button and select *Animation Settings* from the list that appears. In the *Build Options* section, select *Build* from the drop-down list and select *Start when previous build ends.* This will make each picture appear automatically one after the other. Choose an option from the *Effects* section to make a picture move onto the screen in a particular way.

Use this technique to set an effect for each of the pictures. When you have finished, select *Slide Show* from the *View* menu. Select *All* in the *Slide* section and *Manual Advance* in the *Advance* section. Then click on *Show.*

The Animation Settings box

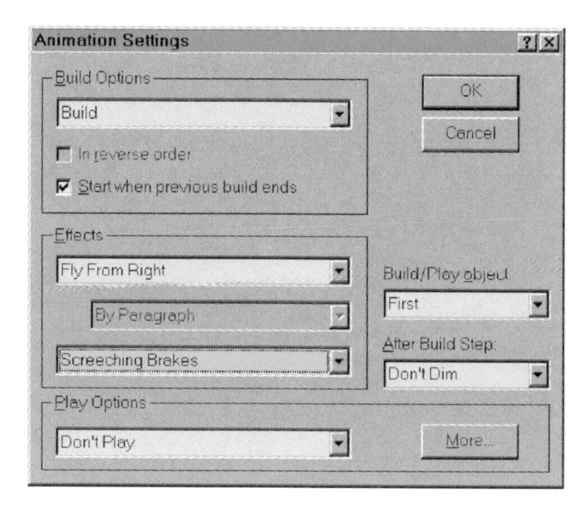

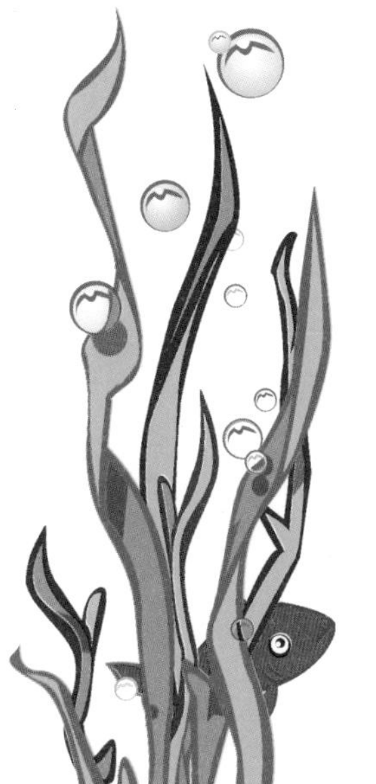

When you start the show, your fish will whizz on one by one to build up a crowded undersea scene.

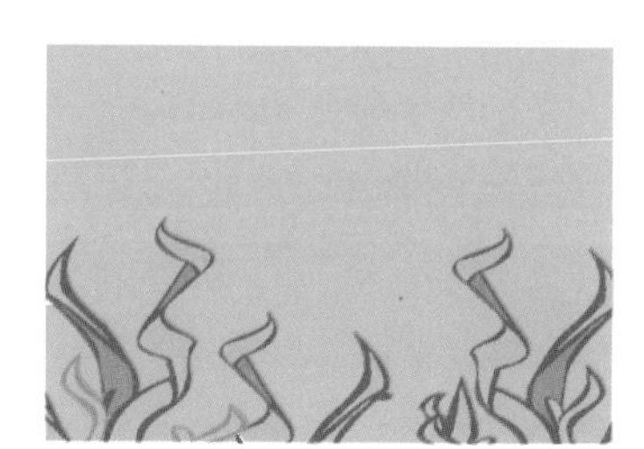

The World Wide Web, also known as the Web, is the most accessible part of the Internet (see page 48). It contains millions of documents crammed with information on all kinds of subjects. These documents are stored on computers all over the world. They appear on your screen in the form of pages called Web pages. A group of Web pages created by a particular organization is called a site.

In this section, you'll discover how to find your way around the Web. This is known as browsing. Find out what's available on it by taking an imaginary trip around the world and looking at a selection of Web pages.

Before you can use the Web, you need the right equipment and software (see page 62). This can be expensive. So, if you are not already connected, try it out first at school, a local library, or at an Internet Café where you pay to use an Internet connection.

69 LOOK AT A WEB PAGE

To look at Web pages, you need a program called a browser (see page 62). You view the contents of a Web page in your browser's window.

Each Web page has a unique address which tells your computer exactly where to find it. To view a page for which you have an address, connect up to the Internet and launch your browser. Type the address in a box in your browser's window. It is usually called something like the *Location, Go To* or *Address* box, depending on which browser you are using.

Try typing the address below in the relevant box in your browser's window. Then press the Return key or click on the confirmation button (usually called *Send, OK* or *Go)*. A *Freezone* Web page will be displayed. It may take some time to appear. If it's taking too long, you can stop the page fróm loading by clicking on the *Stop* button on your browser's *Toolbar*. If you have problems, try typing the address again.

If you want to speed things up a little, switch off the images, so that when you view a Web page your computer only loads text. In *Internet Explorer,* you do this by selecting *Options* on the *View* menu. Select the *General* tab and switch off the *Show pictures* option. If everything else fails, try browsing the Web at a different time of day when it might be less busy.

Type this Web address in your browser's window.

A Web browser called Internet Explorer

Web pages are displayed here.

70 EXPLORE THE WEB

You can look at Web pages even if you don't have the address of a particular page. Sometimes it's more fun just to look around and see what you find. Almost all Web pages contain special links called hyperlinks. These connect Web pages together, allowing you to jump from one page to another by clicking on them. When you move your pointer over a hyperlink, it will change to a different pointer shape. Each time you click on a hyperlink, you have to wait for a new page to appear in your browser's window before continuing.

Hyperlinks appear as small pictures, or coloured or underlined text.

When you connect to the Internet and launch your browser, a particular page, called a *Start* page, will automatically appear in your browser's window. This is usually your service provider's (see page 62) home page, which is like a contents page. You can use this as a starting point for exploring the Web.

Once you have looked through a few Web pages, you can use the *Back* button to look back at the pages you have already viewed or the *Forward* button to move forward again.

71 SEARCH THE WEB

If you don't have the address of a Web page, you can use a facility called a search service to look for Web pages on a particular subject. Your Web browser should have a *Search* button which enables you to view a list of search services. Click on one to go to that page.

Popular search services

Most search services allow you to type in a key word which describes the subject you want to look up. You will need to follow the instructions given by a service to find out exactly what you need to type.

Go to a search service to try a key word search. Keep the description simple and use the singular form of the word. For example, if you wanted to search for pages about tigers, you would type the key word **tiger** in the *Search* box. You then click on a button to start the search. A list of pages containing the word tiger will appear. Find a page that sounds interesting and click on its hyperlink to look at it.

The* Yahooligans *search service is especially for kids: http://www.yahooligans.com/.

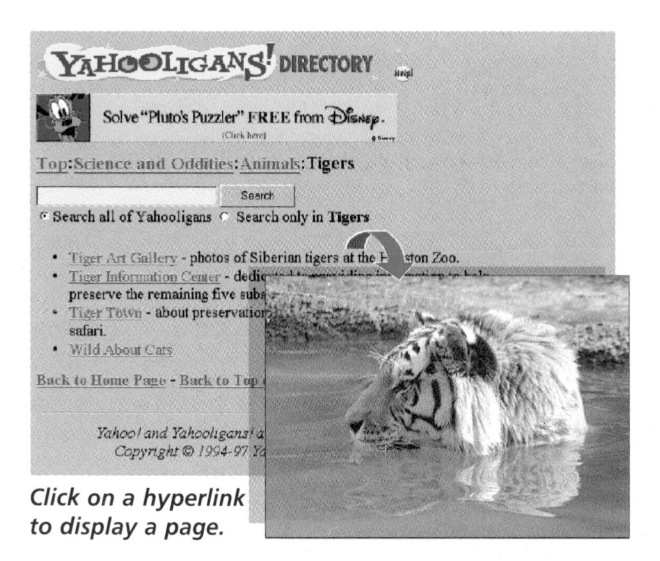

Click on a hyperlink to display a page.

72 VISIT THE WHITE HOUSE

Lots of museums and other interesting places have sites on the Web. You can take a tour of a building, look at photographs and read interesting information about the place. Some sites even have maps that you can click on to jump to pictures of different rooms in a building.

Use your search skills (see projects 70 and 71) to help you visit the American President at home in the White House. There is a special site for kids where you can find out about the history of the White House and some of the children and pets that have lived there. You could even send e-mail to the President (see project 81 for advice on sending e-mail).

The White House For Kids

73 USE A PAINTING AS WALLPAPER

In project 35, you discovered how to design your own wallpaper to cover your computer's desktop. If your own artistic efforts were not very good, why not use a famous work of art instead?

Use the search method described in project 71 to find your way to the Web pages of the Louvre museum, Paris. Browse around the site by clicking on hyperlinks. When you find a picture you would like to use, click on it with the right-hand mouse button and select *Set as Wallpaper* from the list that appears. Alternatively, you could use the technique described in project 35 to save and name the picture and then set it as wallpaper using the method described in project 34.

This picture of the Mona Lisa was obtained from the Louvre museum.

74 GET UP-TO-DATE INFORMATION

The Web is useful for getting up-to-date information on all kinds of subjects. You can find out the latest football results, what's top of the music charts and what's on TV.

You can get this kind of information about places all over the world. So if you're planning a trip somewhere (or you just want to know more about a particular country or city), you can use the Web to find out everything you need to know before you go. It's much more useful than an out-of-date guide book. Use your browsing and search skills to see what you can discover about Hong Kong. Can you find out what the weather is like there right now?

From satellite images to tourist information, it's all there on the Web.

75 SEND A POSTCARD

When you go away on holiday, it's nice to send postcards to your friends. You can do the same thing on your tour of the Web. There are postcard sites where you can choose from a selection of pictures in the postcard "shop" and then add your own message to it. Use the search method described in project 71 to look for a postcard site. Try the key word **postcard**.

Each site will have instructions telling you exactly what to do. You'll need to choose a picture, type in your message and the e-mail address of the person you want to send the postcard to (see project 81). Then click on the relevant button or hyperlink to send it.

When you send a postcard, it's not delivered directly to your friend's e-mail address, but is kept at a storage address instead. A computer called a postmaster then sends a message to your friend to say that there is a postcard waiting for them at a particular address. Your friend can then take a look at the card by visiting that address. Postcards are usually stored there for about two weeks, before being deleted.

76 READ A MAGAZINE

Take a break on your tour of the Web by relaxing with an on-line magazine. Lots of ordinary magazines and newspapers now have their own Web pages, but there are also lots of on-line magazines, sometimes called e-zines, that only exist on the Web. There are magazines especially for kids too. Many of these welcome articles from readers of all ages. So you could write in and tell people all about your experiences on the Web.

Alternatively, you could just sit back and read what other people have written. You'll find stories, film reviews, facts about popstars, letters, puzzles - everything an ordinary magazine has and more. Use the search technique described in project 71 to hunt for magazines sites. Try the key word **magazine**. Then find one that sounds interesting and take a look at it.

A selection of material from Web magazines

Projects 72 to 76 involved looking at lots of different Web pages. Now you can find out how to produce a Web page of your own. You can include anything you want: information about yourself, a band you like, or a hobby. If you work through the projects in this section, you'll find out how to plan, create and publish your own Web page.

77 PLAN A WEB PAGE

You should plan a layout for your page before you turn it into a Web page. First, look at personal home pages on the Web for ideas for what to include (see project 71 for advice on searching the Web). Be careful about the personal information you include on your Web page. See page 48 for advice on Internet safety.

Sketch a layout for your page on a piece of paper. Make a note of any pictures you want to include (see project 87 for advice on obtaining pictures). Do you want to have hyperlinks (see project 70) to other Web pages? If so, note down the addresses of the pages you want to be connected to. You might also want to include your e-mail address (see project 81) so that people can write to you.

A Web page sketch

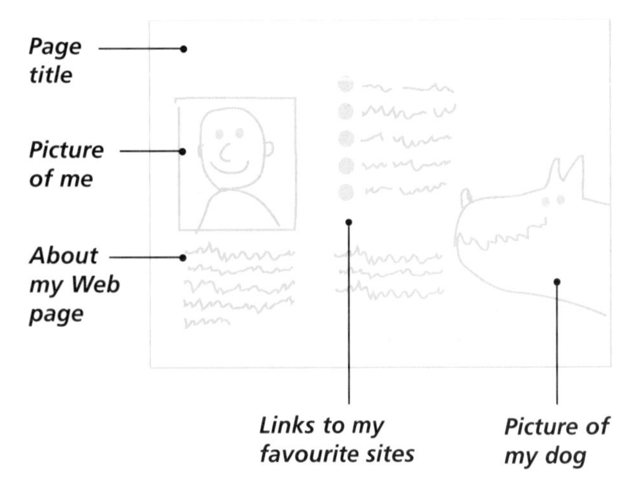

78 BUILD A WEB PAGE

The easiest way to arrange, or build, a Web page is by using a program called a Web editor. Many of these are suitable for complete beginners. Your service provider may supply one. If not, there are lots on the Web (see project 88 for advice on downloading programs), or you could buy one from a shop. It's a good idea to try out a program with a free trial period to check that it's easy enough for you to use.

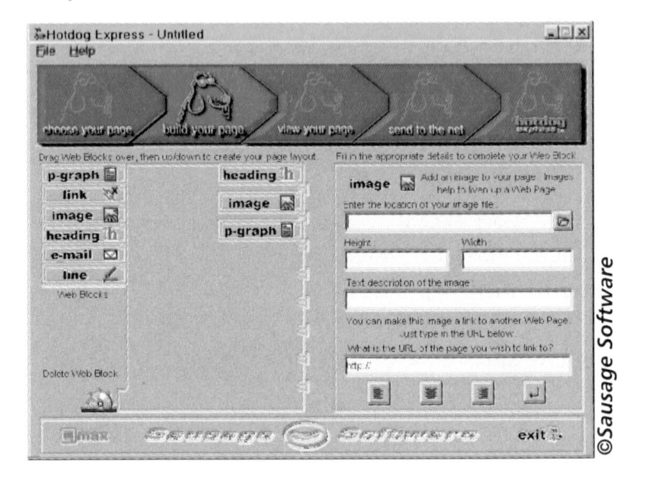

This Web editor is called Hotdog Express. It's available at http://www.sausage.com/.

With most simple Web editors, you build up a page by selecting the type of item you want to include and then supplying more details about it. For example, to add text, you select the text option. Usually a box appears and you can type in your text and choose from different font sizes and styles. If you select the link option, you'll need to type in the address of the Web page that you want to link your page to. Add background colours, pictures and headings using the same technique.

Find a Web editor that you like and transform your plan (see project 77) into a Web page. If you want to learn about more advanced Web page design, you'll need to find out about HTML (see project 79).

79 TRY OUT HTML

All Web pages are created using a special code called HTML (Hypertext MarkUp Language). This is a set of instructions that tells a browser (see project 69) what colours, fonts and pictures to use for the page. Even Web editors use HTML. They turn the selections that you make when you click on different buttons into HTML. In this project, you can find out about HTML and use it to produce a very simple Web page.

HTML instructions are called tags and appear in special brackets like these **< >**. Most instructions need a part at the beginning and at the end of the text that the instruction will affect. The part at the end has an extra stroke like this **</ >**.

To type in the code for your Web page, launch *WordPad* and create a new document. Type in the tags exactly as shown in the window at the top of the page. Make up your own text for the parts that aren't in tag brackets. When you have finished, select *Save As* from the *File* menu and name your document **webpage.htm**. In the *Save as type* box, select *Text document*.

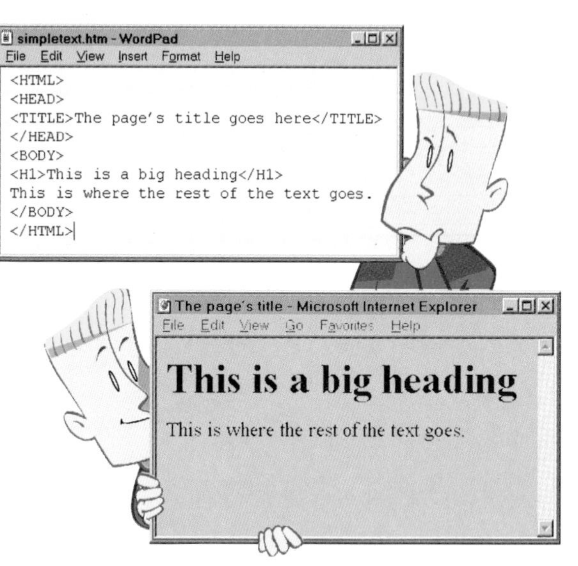

The instructions in the top window will create a Web page like the one in the second window.

To look at your Web page, open your browser window. Select *Open* from the *File* menu and then find and open the document.

You can improve your basic page by adding tags for hyperlinks, pictures and colours. Find out more about HTML at the following sites:
http://members.aol.com/teachemath/create.htm
http://www.smplanet.com/webpage/webpage.html.

80 PUT YOUR PAGE ON THE WEB

Once you've created a page, you need to put it on the Web so that other people can look at it. Most service providers will allow you to do this free of charge. If they offer this service, they should give you on-line help telling you exactly how to go about it. You will then be given an address, or URL, for your page. You then need to "upload" or copy your page to that address. Once you have done this, your page will be on the Web.

To make sure that other Web users visit your page, you need to tell them that it's there. The best way to do this is to register it with a search service (see project 71). Try registering it with the Yahooligans! search service. Go to **http://www.yahooligans.com/** and click on *Add Site*. Type in details about your Web page on the form and then click on *Submit*.

The Add Site icon in Yahooligans!

Web addresses often change. So if you have included hyperlinks on your Web page, you'll need to update the addresses now and again, or the hyperlinks won't work. Your service provider should provide information about how to do this.

The Internet is a network made up of millions of computers all over the world which are connected together so that they can exchange information. On pages 42 to 45, you toured the World Wide Web, the best-known and most user-friendly part of the Internet. In this section, you can find out about other Internet facilities. Turn to page 62 for advice about the equipment you need.

81 SEND A MESSAGE

You can send electronic messages, called e-mail, to anyone else with an Internet connection. Everyone on the Internet has a unique e-mail address, like a personal mailbox, where they can send and receive messages.

To send e-mail, you need an e-mail program. Most service providers (see page 62) supply one of these with your initial Internet software package. Launch your e-mail program. Click on the menu option or button that allows you to compose a new message. In the window that appears, type your message and the address of the person you want to send it to. To send your e-mail, connect up to the Internet and click on the *Send* button. Disconnect when your message has been sent.

An e-mail window

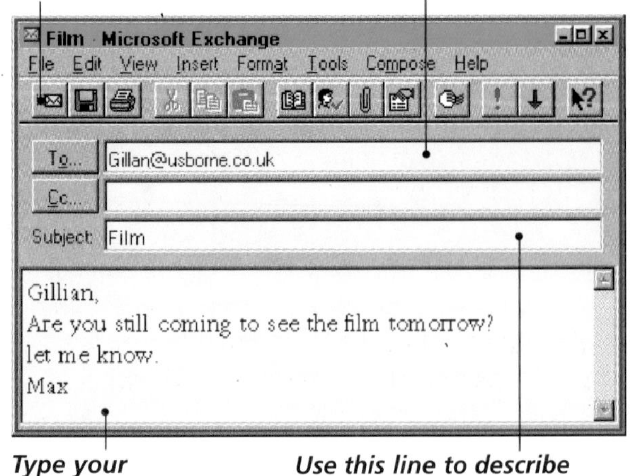

82 FIND AN E-PAL

If you want to send an e-mail (see project 81), but don't have anyone to send one to, what you need is an e-pal. An e-pal is like a penfriend, except that instead of writing letters you exchange e-mail messages.

There are lots of Web sites offering e-pals. You could search for one using the method described in project 71, or take a look at the Freezone E-pals site below. On these sites, you can reply to advertisements placed by other people, or you can fill in a form about yourself to advertise for e-pals. Read the Internet Safety box below before you do this, and make sure you read the site's rules or guidelines about exchanging e-mails.

Find an e-pal at http://www.freezone.com/epals.

INTERNET SAFETY

In many countries, there are telephone charges and service charges for the time you are on-line (connected to the Internet). So you should always ask permission from the person who pays these charges before you connect up.

Occasionally, you may come across unpleasant material or people on the Internet. If you see or read something you don't like, the best thing to do is simply to avoid it. Always be careful about the personal information you reveal. Never give your address, telephone number, school name, or any other information that you wouldn't want a stranger to know, and never agree to meet anyone in person.

83 JOIN A NEWSGROUP

The Internet is a good way of making contact with people who share your interests. A part of the Internet called USENET is made up of thousands of interest groups called newsgroups, where enthusiasts can read and send articles on particular subjects. To access USENET, you need a program called a newsreader. Your service provider may supply one, or your browser (see project 69) may include a newsreader facility.

Connect up to the Internet and open your newsreader window. Select the menu option that allows you to view a list of newsgroups. To join, or "subscribe", to one, select the box beside its name and click on *Subscribe*. Next time you open your newsreader, select the option that allows you to view the groups that you've subscribed to. Double-click on a newsgroup name to see the articles it contains. Then double-click on an article name to read it. Read a newsgroup's guidelines to find out how you can send in articles of your own.

Double-click on the name of a newsgroup to see the articles it contains.

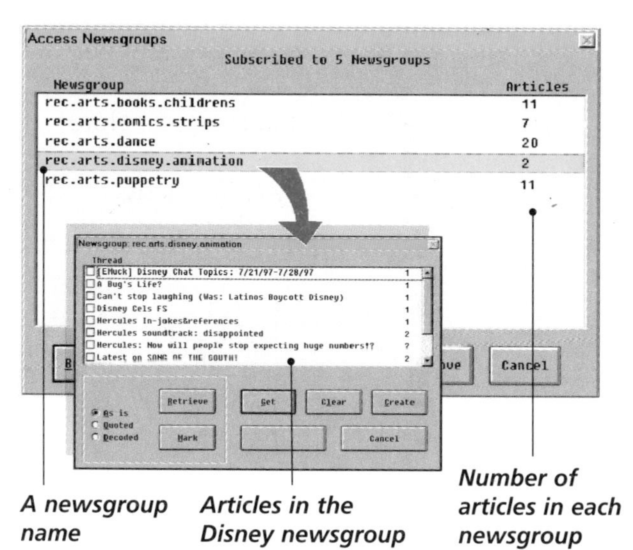

A newsgroup name

Articles in the Disney newsgroup

Number of articles in each newsgroup

84 SUBSCRIBE TO A MAILING LIST

Mailing lists are similar to newsgroups (see project 83), except that you receive messages by e-mail instead of searching for articles that interest you. It's one way of making sure you get lots of interesting e-mail.

You can find a list of mailing lists at **http://www.liszt.com**, or you could use the search method described in project 71 to look for interesting ones. Double-click on the name of a mailing list to find out more about it, and to see what you need to do to subscribe to that list. Usually you'll need to send a short e-mail message (see project 81) to a mailing list controller. This will then mean that you are automatically enrolled.

A list of mailing lists

Once you have subscribed, you should receive an e-mail telling you more about the list. You should keep this message for future reference: it may tell you how to unsubscribe, in case you should want to stop receiving messages. All the messages that are sent to the mailing list will be sent to your e-mail address. Then you can read them, as with any e-mail message. Some mailing lists also allow you to send messages to other members.

85 GET HOMEWORK HELP

There are special homework Web sites on the Internet where you can get personal help on all kinds of subjects. You could join in a debate about a book you're reading, or get help solving a difficult maths problem. On many sites teachers are available to answer your questions and to help you to research projects. To see a list of homework sites, click on the *Homework Answers* hyperlink in the *School Bell* section of *Yahooligans!* (see project 71).

86 PLAY ON-LINE GAMES

You can play "on-line games" live via the Internet. Whenever you make a move, it will immediately be transmitted to the screens of your opponents, who could be any of the millions of Internet users around the world. You can play traditional games, such as chess, or play a character in an amazing fantasy world.

To play on-line games, you need a piece of software called a client program. Most games pages have hyperlinks to pages where you can download suitable software (see project 88).

A screen from a game called The Realm, where each character is being played by an Internet user. http://www.realmserver.com/demo.html

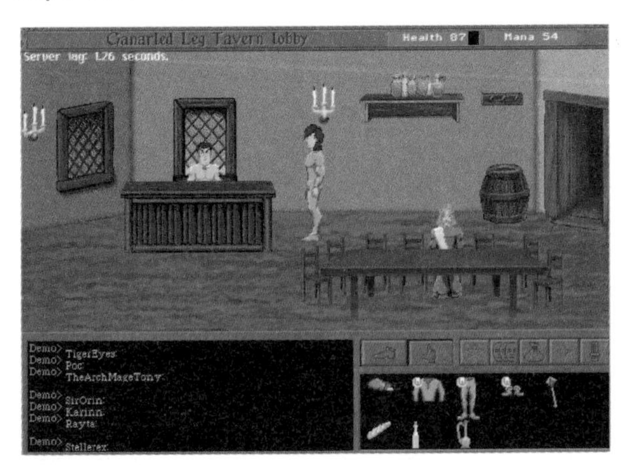

87 MAKE A MULTIMEDIA LIBRARY

Just as you can copy programs from the Internet (see project 88), you can also copy pictures, sounds, animations and video clips. You could collect a selection of images or sounds to use in some of the projects in this book. Launch the *Windows®* *Explorer* program and select *New* and then *Folder* from the *File* menu. Name the folder **Multimedia Library**.

In most browsers, to copy, or download, a picture you have found on the Web, click on it with your right mouse button and select *Save Image to Disk* from the list that appears. Find and select your *Multimedia Library* folder and click on *OK*. The picture will then be copied into that folder. To copy sound or video clips, you use the same method. But instead of clicking on the image, you need to click on the hyperlink that represents the file. Video clips are like short films. They can take a long time to download, and you may need a viewer program to look at them.

Many of the things that you download from the Internet belong to people. If you want to use them for something public, such as a magazine, make sure you get permission. Alternatively, search for "copyright free" images, for which you don't need permission.

These copyright free pictures were obtained from http:// www.havanastreet.com.

88 GET FREE PROGRAMS

There is a huge range of software available on the Internet for you to copy, or download, onto your computer. You can download games, screen savers, drawing programs and programs for using the Internet.

You can obtain "freeware" programs free of charge. With "shareware" programs, you may have to pay a small fee to use them, although many of these have free trial periods.

Visit the Children's Software site at: http://www.gamesdomain.com/tigger/.

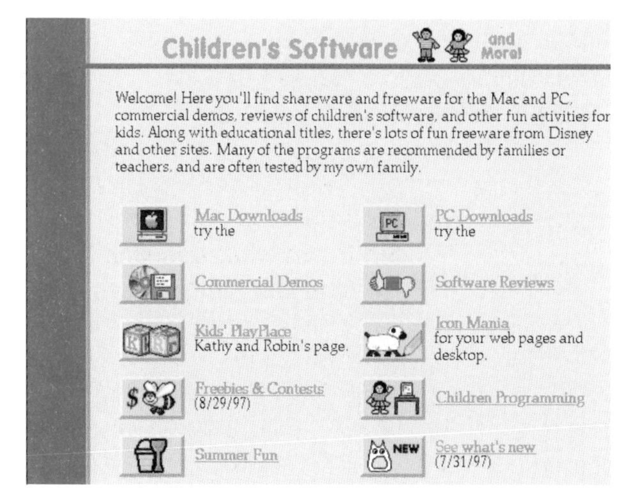

When you find a program you want to download, you can usually click on a hyperlink to start the downloading process. The file may start to download immediately. Alternatively, a dialog box may appear, asking you to specify where to copy it - for example, onto your computer's hard disk or onto a floppy disk.

It can take several hours to download large files. Sometimes large files are compressed, or zipped, to make them smaller. You may need to use a program to unzip them again ready for use. Whenever you copy Internet files, there is a risk that you may accidentally copy a program called a "virus". A virus can damage the programs and data on your computer. Guard against viruses by making sure that your computer has up-to-date "anti-virus" software.

89 HAVE AN ON-LINE CHAT

A fun way of communicating with other Internet users is to join in an on-line chat. You "chat" by typing in messages. To have an on-line chat, also known as an Internet Relay Chat (IRC), you need a program called an IRC client. Your service provider may supply one of these, or you can download one from the Internet (see project 88).

To join in a chat, you need to enter a "chat room". This is a place that is allocated to a chat on a particular subject. Only visit chat rooms that state that they are suitable for kids. Use the *Yahooligans!* search service (see project 71) to search for them. Some chats are supervised. This means that someone will check that no unsuitable material appears. Read the chat room's rules and guidelines before you go in.

When you enter a chat room, there may be people using it already. Usually there will be a *Listen* or *Preview* button that you can click on to find out what they are saying. You then communicate with them by typing in a message and clicking on a button to "say" it. Your message will appear on the screens of the other people using the chat room.

Try out Freezone's Chat Box at http://chat.freezone.com.

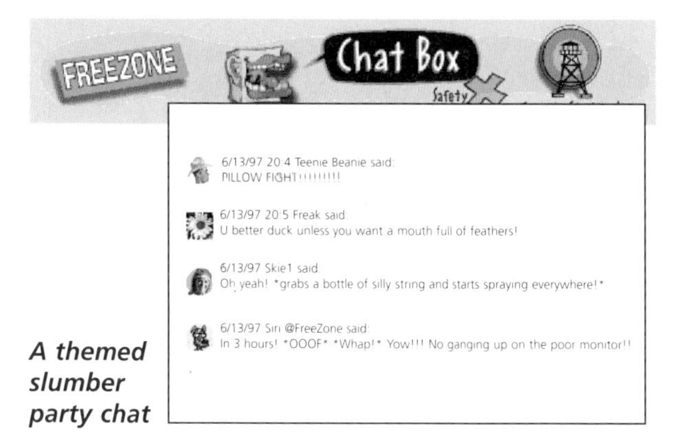

A themed slumber party chat

A program is a set of instructions that tells a computer what to do. In this book, you have used lots of different programs to create things. Some programs such as *Microsoft® Access* and *Word* allow you to write mini programs called macros. These are written in a code called Visual Basic. In this section, you can find out how to program a picture of a plane to fly, and make a message box appear when it lands.

90 FLY A PLANE

You can write a macro program which will move a plane picture each time you click on a button. To do this, launch *Access*. Select *Blank Database* and click on *OK*. Name your database **Fly.mdb** and click on *Create*.

Select the *Forms* tab and click on *New*. Then choose *Design View* and click on *OK*. A *Form* window containing a grid will appear. Click and drag the bottom right corner of the grid to make it fill the window.

Select *Toolbox* on the *View* menu in the main window. Click on the *Command Button* option, as shown below. Move your pointer to the bottom right corner of the grid and click and drag to draw a button. Then click in the middle of the button. Delete the existing text and type **Fly**.

The Toolbox

Toolbox

Command button

Click on the top left corner of the button and select *Properties* from the *View* menu. In the box that appears, select the *Other* tab. Type **FlyButton** in the *Name* box and close the *Command Button* box.

Draw another command button beside the first one. Select the new button and select *Properties* from the *View* menu. Select the *Other* tab and type **PlaneButton** in the *Name* box. Then select the *Format* tab. Click in the *Picture* box and click on the dots at the right of the box. Select *Airplane* in the *Available Pictures* box and click on *OK*. A picture will be added to the button. Close the *Command Button* box. Minimize the *Form* window.

In the *Database* window, select the *Macros* tab and click on *New*. A window will appear. This is where you tell your computer what each button does. Open the drop-down list on the first line of the *Action* column and select *SetValue*. In the *Item* box below the grid, type **PlaneButton.left**. Type **FlyButton.left*rnd** in the *Expression* box.

On the second line of the *Action* column, choose *SetValue* again. Type **PlaneButton.top** in its *Item* box and **FlyButton.top*rnd** in the *Expression* box. Select *Save As* from the *File* menu in the main window. Type **FlyMacro** in the *New Name* box and click on *OK*.

Maximize your *Form* window and select the *Fly* button. Select *Properties from the View* menu and click on the *Event* tab. Open the drop-down list in the *On Click* box and select *FlyMacro*. Close the box. Select *Save As* from the *File* menu and name the form **Planeform**. Then click on *OK*.

Select the *Forms* tab in the *Fly: Database* window and click on *Open*. A window containing your buttons will appear.

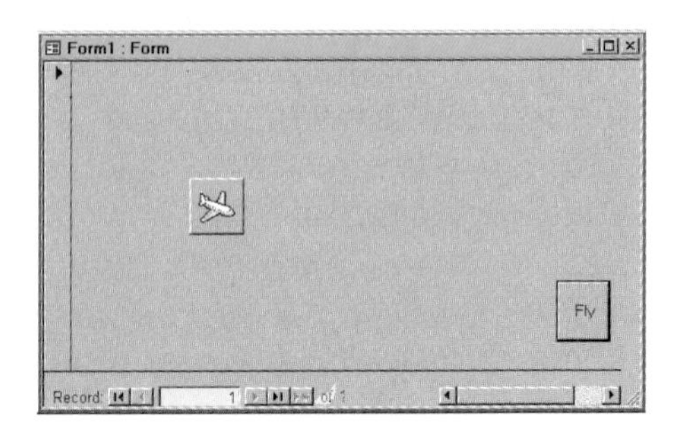

Click on the Fly button to move the plane around.

91 LAND A PLANE

By adding extra instructions to the form you created in project 90, you can program a button to land your plane.

Launch *Access* and open the *Fly.mdb* database. Click on the *Forms* tab. Select *Planeform* and click on *Design*. Draw a command button beside the *Fly* button using the technique described in project 90. Click in the middle of the new button and type **Land**. Select the button and then click on *Properties* on the *View* menu. Select the *Other* tab and type the name **LandButton** in the *Name* box. Close the box and minimize the form.

A Command Button box

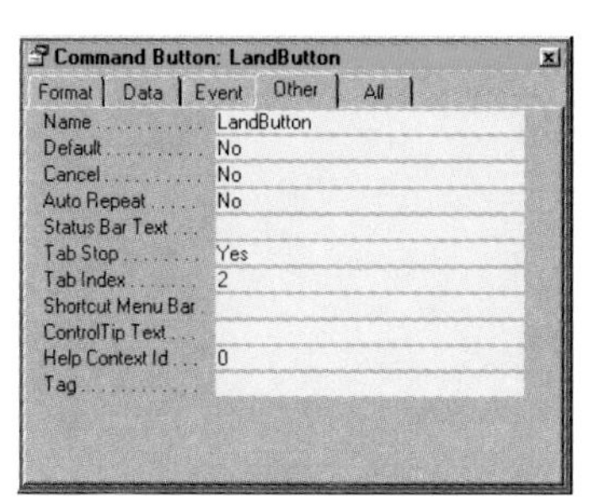

Select the *Macros* tab in the *Database* window and click on *New*. Select *SetValue* from the drop-down list in the *Action* column. Type **PlaneButton.top** in the *Item* box and **FlyButton.top** in the *Expression* box. Select *Save As* from the *File* menu. Type the name **LandMacro** in the *New Name* box and click on *OK*. Then close the *Macro* window.

Maximize your *Form* window and select the *Land* button. Click on *Properties* on the *View* menu. Select the *Event* tab and click in the *OnClick* box. Select LandMacro. Close the *Command Button* box. Save the changes to your form design and then close its window.

In the *Database* window, click on the *Forms* tab. Select the name of your form and click on *Open*. You can click on the *Fly* button to make the plane fly around as you did in project 90. But when you click on the *Land* button, the plane will automatically return to a landing position at the bottom of the form.

92 MAKE A MESSAGE BOX APPEAR

Arrange for a message to appear when your plane lands (see project 91).

Launch *Access* and open the *Fly.mbd* database. Click on the *Macros* tab. Select *LandMacro* and then click on *Design*. Click in an empty box in the *Action* column. Open the drop-down list and select *MsgBox*. Click in the *Message* box below the grid and type the message that you want to appear, for example **Landing successful**. Click in the *Beep* box and select *Yes* from the drop-down list. This tells your computer to make a beeping noise when the message box appears. Save the macro and then close its box.

Click on the *Forms* tab in the *Database* window. Select the name of your form and then click on *Open*. This time when you click on the *Land* button, your plane will land and a message box like the one below will appear. A beep will sound as the box appears.

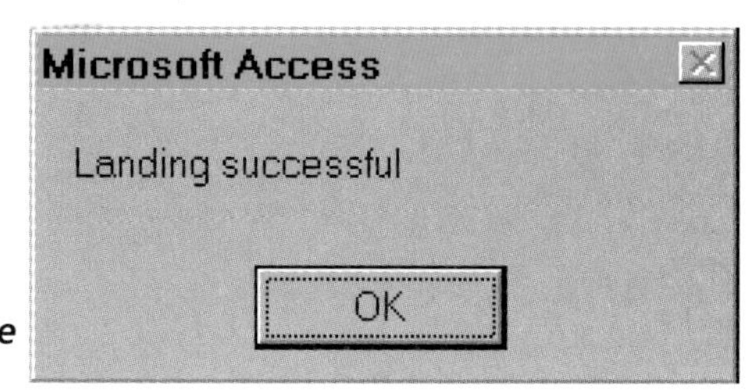

A message box

The programs in this section all offer fun ways of using your computer to invent or participate in imaginary worlds. They are a little like games, but they have a more serious side, involving programming and decision-making.

93 BUILD YOUR OWN TOWN

One of the most interesting kinds of simulation is a form of strategy game where you build and run your own town, country or imaginary world. Some of the most popular simulations of this kind are produced by a company called Maxis. You can find out more about their simulations on the Internet at **http://www.maxis.com**.

The example screen below is from a program called *SimTown*. In this, you develop your own town, choose the characters that live in it, and decide what kinds of buildings it will have. Your decisions will affect how the town develops. It may be fun to build lots of pizza restaurants and cinemas, but you'll also need roads for the residents of your town to get around. By watching the consequences of your actions, you can change your tactics to make your town run smoothly.

A screen from SimTown

94 VISIT A VIRTUAL WORLD

Virtual Reality is a term given to an imaginary environment, created using computer graphics, which gives a sensation of reality. The picture below shows a Virtual Reality arcade game. The equipment transmits information about your movements, which affects an image displayed on a screen inside your headset. For example, when you look down, the scene on the screen will show the ground.

A Virtual Reality arcade game

You can get headsets similar to the one above to attach to your own computer. But the best way to try out Virtual Reality at home is by using a program called a simulator. The most common simulator programs are ones which recreate the experience of flying a plane or driving a car. Although you're not surrounded by pictures as you are when you wear a headset, the pictures on your computer's screen will still change as you move, for example when you overtake other cars, or when you move your joystick to land the plane.

Screens from Microsoft® Flight Simulator 98

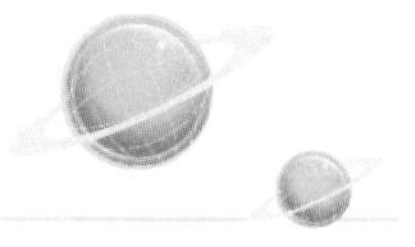

95 PROGRAM YOUR OWN WORLD

You can use a program called *MicroWorlds* to produce a mini world like the one below. You can download a demonstration version of *MicroWorlds* (see project 88) from **http://www.lcsi.ca.**

Your scene, or "world", will behave according to certain rules which you will develop. You begin by instructing a basic "turtle" character to move around your screen. This can then be transformed into all kinds of interesting characters.

A MicroWorlds world

Tool Palette ***Command Center***

When you launch *MicroWorlds,* a picture of a turtle will appear in the middle of the page. Select the *Magnifier* button and click on the turtle several times to enlarge it. You can rotate the turtle by selecting the *Arrow* button and then dragging the turtle's head. Turn it to face the left. To program the turtle, click on the *Eye* button and then click on the turtle. A programming box will appear.

A turtle

Arrow button

Magnifier button

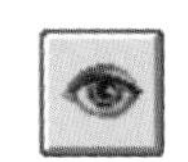

Eye button

Each turtle has a unique name which appears in the *Name* section of its programming box. For example, the turtle in the box below is called t1. Use the *Instruction* box to type in the command that tells the turtle what to do. For example, **fd 5** tells the turtle to move forward 5 spaces. Select the *Once* option and click on *OK.*

A programming box for giving a turtle instructions

Each time you click on the turtle, it will move in the way that you have programmed it to. Once you have programmed a turtle, you can change its shape. Click on the *Dog* button in the *Command Center.* You can then choose a picture from the *Shapes Center.* Select one of the pair of dogs and click on the turtle on the page to change it to the selected picture.

You can choose a picture from the Shapes Center.

Dog button

You can make the dog run by alternating between the pair of dog pictures. To do this, select the *Eye* button and click on the dog on the page. Type **setshape "dog1 fd 2 setshape "dog2 fd 2** in the *Instruction* box. Select *Many Times* and then click on *OK.* When you click on the dog on the page it will run across the screen. Click on it again and it will stop running.

You can program a dog to run across your screen.

Computers are developing at an amazing rate. In this section you can find out about some of the more unusual and advanced possibilities that are available to computer users. You may not have access to the programs and equipment to try out all of these things. However, you might be able to try them out at a computer showroom, or you can find out more about them on the Internet.

96 MAKE A MATHEMATICAL PICTURE

You can use mathematical formulae to produce beautifully intricate images called fractals. With their luminous colours and swirling patterns, they often look like fantasy landscapes.

They are made from equations like the one below. When the letters are replaced with certain numbers, these are interpreted as curves and points in a 3D picture.

An example equation
$z = kz^2 + c$

Try producing your own fractals at **http://zenith.berkeley.edu/seidel/Frac/**. (If you can't find this site, use the technique described in project 71 to search for similar ones.) This site has a Test Fractal Generator, where you can type in numbers to produce your own fractal art. Each box contains a default value. Try changing these numbers by a small amount. (*Value of a* and *Value of b* are good ones to change.)

Choose a value from the list labelled *Size of x,y field in pixels*. The larger sizes will take longer to calculate. Click on the *Crank it Up* button to see the fractal produced by your numbers. If you don't produce an interesting image at first, keep trying different numbers to see what effect they have.

Fractal images from http://sprott.physics.wisc.edu/carlson.htm

97 SCAN IN PICTURES

You can change ordinary photographs or magazine pictures into "digital" images which can then be used by your computer. You could put a photograph of yourself on your headed notepaper, create a calendar using your holiday snapshots, or have a photograph of your pet as your desktop wallpaper. You can even have fun distorting the pictures (see project 98).

You can copy any image that appears on paper onto your computer using a device called a scanner. There are lots of different kinds of scanners, most of which are quite expensive. But, you can buy small scanners that are suitable for scanning in photographs. There are also lots of printing shops which have scanners where you can pay to have a picture scanned.

To use a scanner, you lift up the lid and place your picture face down.

One way of creating digital photographs is by using a digital camera, which you can then link directly to your computer. Alternatively, some photo processing stores may be able to develop your photographs onto a floppy disk for you.

A digital camera looks like an ordinary camera, but doesn't need film.

98 HAVE FUN WITH PHOTOS

You can use photographs that you have taken yourself to make all kinds of impressive things. There are lots of programs which allow you to work with photographs. One of the simplest is a program called *Adobe® PhotoDeluxe™*.

The *PhotoDeluxe™* program includes a number of set activities. These offer step-by-step instructions for projects such as making cards, calendars and amazing collages using photographs. It even supplies a number of digital images for you to work with. If you want to use pictures of your own, look at project 97 to find out how you can do this.

The unusual collages below were made by adding a head from one photo onto a body in another. To create this effect, you simply cut out the head and rub out any background on the section surrounding the head. Then place it in the position you want on the photograph containing the body. If you use your own photographs, you could transform your friends and family into weird and wonderful creatures.

A selection of things you can make by following PhotoDeluxe's guided activities

You don't need to follow the guided activities. Click on the *On Your Own* button to experiment with the different techniques yourself. You can distort and rotate pictures, add "motion blur" to create a sense of movement, make new pictures look old and do all kinds of other things. First you need to get the picture you want to work with. Then select an area of the picture and click on one of the modifying buttons to see what effect it has.

You can make amazing body collages like these by following one of PhotoDeluxe's guided activities.

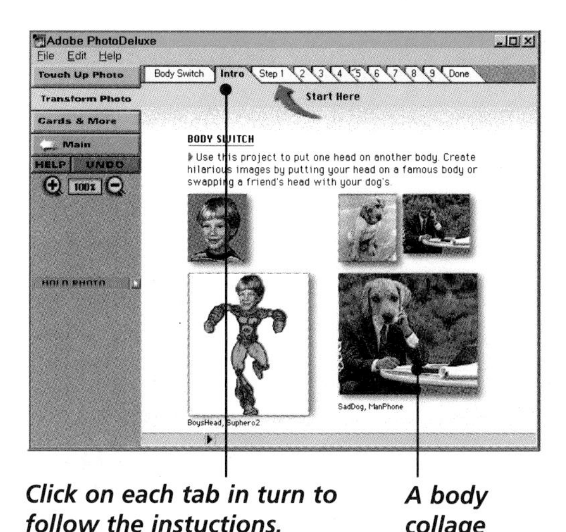

The On Your Own facility allows you to experiment with special effects yourself.

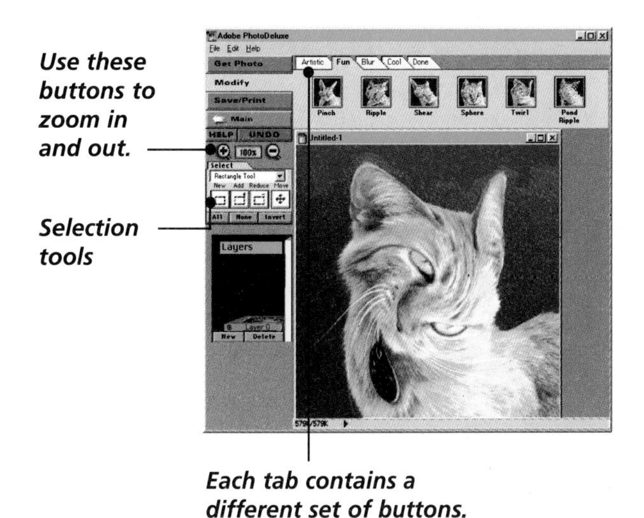

99 TALK TO YOUR COMPUTER

There are speech recognition programs available which enable you to communicate with your computer by speaking to it.

Using a voice-controlled word-processing package, you can enter text into your computer by speaking into a microphone rather than typing. The computer "listens" to what you are saying and then shows on the screen the words that it thinks you said. Because people speak with different accents and at different speeds, you have to teach the computer to recognize your voice. You do this by correcting its mistakes. After a while the computer will start to get better at recognizing your voice and way of speaking.

Computers don't understand what you are saying, but they can recognize the sounds that you make. They can then respond in the way that they have been programmed to. A program called *Microsoft® Agent* allows you to use interactive animated characters, like the ones below, on Web pages and in *Windows®* programs. The characters respond to what you say by performing certain actions. This means that you can use your voice to give your computer instructions.

Find out more about interactive characters at http://www.microsoft.com/workshop/prog/agent.

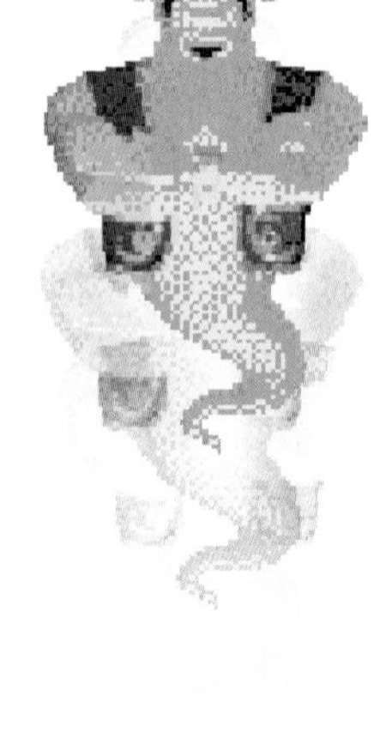

100 MAKE THE NEWS

If you enjoyed making your own newspaper in project 27, try out DeskTop Publishing (DTP). This allows you to use your computer to arrange pictures and text on a page. Most books and magazines that you see will have been produced using a DeskTop Publishing program. They are more advanced than most word-processing programs. For professional results, use a program like *QuarkXPress*$_{TM}$ (see below), or you may be able to find simple "shareware" programs on the Internet (see project 88).

The page shown here was created using a DeskTop Publishing program called QuarkXpress$_{TM}$.

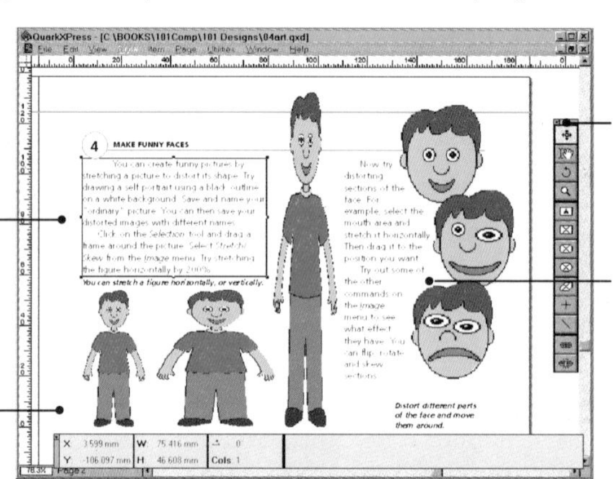

Text appears in boxes which can be arranged in different shapes.

***You can add, or "import", pictures created in programs such as* Paint.**

There are lots of tools to help you lay out a page.

You can "wrap" text around pictures.

101 MORPH AN IMAGE

Morphing is a way of transforming one image into another. Lots of advertisements and films use this technique to create extraordinary special effects. Morphing works by taking certain "key" points on two images and then using these to recreate pictures that are part way between the two.

Morphing was used to produce special effects in the film **The Mask.**

You can try out morphing for yourself with *Gryphon Software's Morph* program. It's easy to use and you can download a demonstration copy (see project 88) from Web site **http://mirror.gryphonsw.com/morph/faq.html#Demos**. If you have difficulty downloading it, look at the site itself for more information.

You could use your own photographs (see project 97) and make a friend turn into a dog before your eyes. However, to start with, try making a morph using the images supplied with the program. When you launch *Morph*, a window like the one below will appear inside a larger window.

Double-click on the first box. In the box that appears, select *photo1.jpg* and click on *OK*. Double-click on the second box, select *photo2.jpeg* and click on *OK*. These will appear as your *Start* and *End* images, which are the images that your morph will be based on.

Morph window

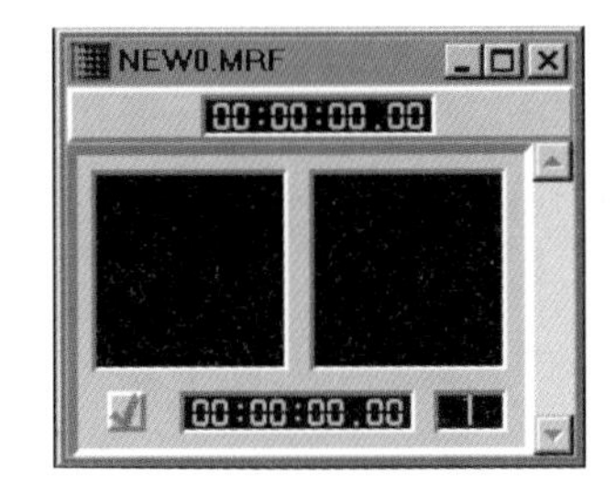

Begin by marking key points on the *Start* image. You need to mark the edges of the faces so that they match up when you morph them. Mark points such as the edges of the mouth and eyes. To do this, select the *Key points* tool and click on the image.

Key points tool

Arrow tool

When you add a point to the *Start* image, a copy appears on the *End* image. Because the heads are different shapes, the copy may appear in a different position. You need to move each point into the equivalent position. For example, if a point marks the top of the right ear in the first picture, move it to the top of the right ear in the second. Click on a point on the *Start* image. The corresponding point on the *End* image will turn red. Using the *Arrow* tool, drag the red point into position. The more points you add, the better your morph will be.

When you have finished, select *Morph Image* from the *Windows* menu. In the window that appears, drag the slider to the halfway point. Then select *Morph* from the *Sequence* menu to morph the two pictures together.

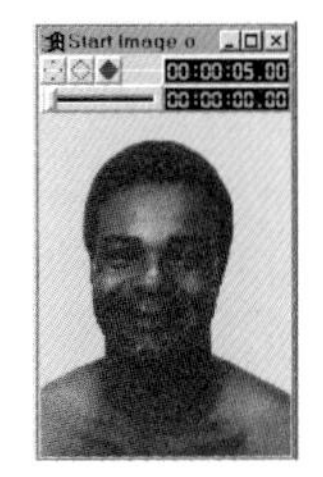

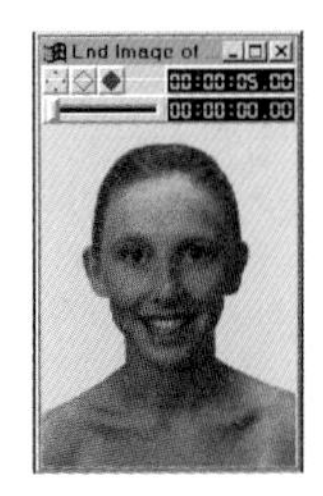

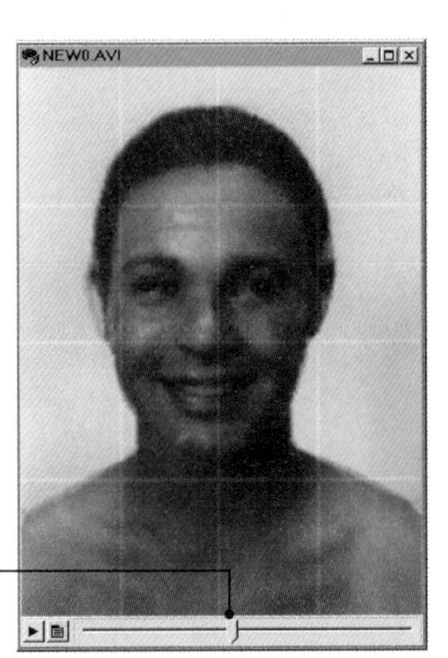

The bottom image is a morph of the images above.

To carry out the projects in this book, you'll need certain programs and equipment. In this section, you can find out more detailed information about what you need. Some alternative programs are also listed. The Internet is a good place to find out about the latest software. There are some useful Web addresses on page 62.

YOUR COMPUTER

Ideally your computer should have a 486 or Pentium chip and at least 16MB of memory. But as long as it is capable of running *Windows® 3.1* or a later version of *Windows®*, you should be able to carry out most of the projects in this book. Additional equipment may be required for specific projects.

You will also need a printer if you want to print out your work. If you don't have a colour printer, see page 8 for tips on improving black and white print-outs.

The programs in this book run on IBM-compatible PCs with versions of the *Microsoft® Windows®* operating system. If you have an Apple Macintosh computer, you'll find that some of the programs mentioned are not available for your computer. But usually you'll be able to find alternative programs of the same general type (for example another word-processing program) that are suitable.

MICROSOFT® WINDOWS®

Many of the instructions in this book relate to *Windows®95*, and the simple programs that are supplied with it. If you have a different version of *Windows®* you will still be able to carry out many of the projects. Some program names are different. For example, in *Windows® 3.1* the equivalent of *Windows® 95*'s *Explorer* program is called *File Manager*. Although the programs are not identical, they do offer similar facilities. Further details of equivalent programs are given on these pages.

MICROSOFT® OFFICE

Microsoft® Office is a collection of programs. Other similar collections of programs include *Lotus® SmartSuite* and *Corel® Office*.

There are several different versions of *Office* which each contain different programs. *Office Professional* includes: *Access* (a database program), *Excel* (a spreadsheet program), *Word* (a word-processing program), *PowerPoint* (a presentation program) and *Schedule+* (a personal organizer program). Other versions may have slightly different programs. But you can buy all these programs individually too.

COMPUTER ART

The instructions given in this section are for the *Paint* program supplied with *Windows® 95*. The equivalent program in *Windows® 3.1* is called *Paintbrush*. Most drawing programs will offer similar kinds of basic facilities. The following simple programs are good for craft type projects: *Fractal Design Dabbler®*, *Print® Artist* from *Sierra, The Print Shop®* and *Kid Pix Studio®* made by Broderbund.

If you want to try a professional graphics program, take a look at *CorelDRAW®*, *Adobe® Illustrator or Lotus® Freelance Graphics®*. These offer a bigger range of features and facilities.

WORKING WITH TEXT

There are lots of word-processing programs available. The more advanced programs have more formatting options. The *NotePad* program supplied with *Windows® 95* is a very simple text editor. But the *WordPad* program, also supplied with *Windows® 95*, has options for changing the layout and style of the text. *Windows® 3.1* has an equivalent word-processing program called *Write*.

More extensive facilities are offered by programs such as *Microsoft® Word, Corel® WordPerfect®* and *Lotus® WordPro®*.

HIDDEN FILES

For the projects in this section, you need to use a word-processing program that allows you to insert files into a document. For some projects you need to use a program called *Object Packager.* This is included with *Windows® 95* and *Windows® 3.1*. For the final projects, more effective results can be achieved if you have a word-processing program, such as *Microsoft® Word,* that allows you to create text boxes.

PERSONALIZE YOUR COMPUTER

If you have an Apple Macintosh computer you can still personalize your display. To choose your own settings, go to the Apple menu and choose the *Control Panel* menu.

COMPUTER DIARIES

The instructions given are for *Microsoft® Schedule+*. There are lots of similar planner programs such as *Lotus® Organizer*. Some diary programs for kids offer more creative possibilities, with ideas for things to write, and quotes and options for creating a personal multimedia scrapbook. Look at *Let's Talk About ME!* (GirlGames Inc./Simon and Schuster).

GETTING ORGANIZED

Microsoft® Access includes Wizards which help you to build up a database. Alternative database programs include *Lotus® Approach* and *Corel® Paradox.*

MAKING CALCULATIONS

Although button and menu names may differ, most spreadsheet programs are quite similar. The instructions in this section describe how to use *Microsoft® Excel*. Other well-known spreadsheet programs are *Lotus® 1-2-3* and *Corel® Quattro® Pro*.

SOUND AND MOVING PICTURES

To work with sound on your computer, you need the following equipment: a microphone, speakers or headphones, and a device called a sound card. Some modern "multimedia" computers will already have this equipment. If your computer doesn't, don't worry. You can use a standard microphone and speakers/headphones with your computer. You need to attach these to your computer first. Many new machines have sockets for this at the front. But on some older machines the sockets are on the sound card itself, usually accessed at the back of the main box.

You can buy sound cards at most computer stores, but you'll need to check which are suitable for use with your computer. A sound card slots inside your computer, so you may need help adding it.

Windows® 95 includes two useful programs for working with sound: *Sound Recorder* and *CD Player.* These programs are not available with *Windows® 3.1*. There are lots of other programs that you can use to edit sounds, some of which are more advanced than others. There are also many general music programs (see project 65).

The instructions for the presentation and animation ideas in projects 66 to 68 relate to *Microsoft® PowerPoint*. If you don't have this program, you could experiment with similar presentation programs such as *Corel® Presentations* or *Lotus® ScreenCam®*.

Alternatively, you could try using a specialist animation program. These usually come with a selection of pictures for you to work with, enabling you to produce impressive results very easily. You can direct your own animated film with *Microsoft® 3D Movie Maker*, or you could animate your own artwork in *Broderbund® Kid Pix Studio*. See also the programs in the *Simple programming* and *Computer worlds* sections of this book to find out how you can program your own animations.

INTERNET EQUIPMENT

Before you can use the Internet, you need a device called a modem and use of a telephone line. The modem plugs into your telephone socket. It converts the information produced by your computer into signals which can be sent along telephone lines.

Modems transmit information at different speeds. Using a high speed modem will cut down the time you spend on-line and reduce any telephone charges. Ideally, you should use a modem which has a speed of at least 28,800 bps (bits per second).

INTERNET ACCESS

Once you have the right equipment, you'll need to pay a company which will then provide access to the Internet. The main companies offering this service are called Internet service providers. Look at Internet magazines to find out what different companies offer. Look out for discounts or free trial periods. The main companies are: *Compuserve, America On-line, UUNet Pipex Ltd, Demon Internet, Netcom.*

Companies called on-line services also provide access to the Internet, in addition to access to their own private network. If you have *Windows® 95,* you could use an on-line service called *Microsoft Network (MSN).*

When looking at companies, find out what programs and facilities they offer and how they charge for their services. Some companies charge a monthly fee regardless of how often you use the facility, whereas others charge according to the time you spend on-line.

Most companies provide all the programs you need in order to use the Internet. This should include a browser, an e-mail program and a newsreader program. Many service providers offer space for you to put your own Web pages on the Web. They may also provide a Web editor program to help you build the pages (see page 46).

SIMPLE PROGRAMMING

The programming in this section involves producing macros. There are lots of different programming codes, or languages, such as C, C++, Pascal, Lisp, Prolog and ADA. These are very complicated. If you do want to get into programming, there are specialist programs such as *MicroWorlds* (see project 95) which will help you to find out about it. If you have an Apple Macintosh computer, try out a program called *Cocoa* (**http://cocoa.apple.com**).

COMPUTER WORLDS

There are lots of different kinds of simulation programs. Look in the games section of your local computer store to find interesting ones.

GOING FURTHER

Here are some alternatives to the programs described in this section:
Fractals: *Fractint* (**http://spanky.triumf.ca/www/fractint/fractint.html**)
Speech recognition: DragonDictate Solo (**http://www.endeavour.co.uk**), IBM VoiceType Simply Speaking (**http://www.software.ibm.com/workgroup/voicetype**), Kurzweil VoicePad Pro (**http://www.talk-systems.com**)
DeskTop Publishing: *Adobe® Pagemaker.*

USEFUL WEB ADDRESSES

Manufacturers
Adobe: **http://www.adobe.com/**
Broderbund: **http://www.broderbund.com/**
Fractal Design Corporation: **http://www.fractal.com/**
Lotus: **http://www.lotus.com/**
Microsoft: **http://www.microsoft.com/**
Netscape: **http://www.netscape.com/**
Sierra: **http://www.sierra.com/**
Vividus: **http://www.vividus.com/**
Shareware sites
CNet Shareware: **http://www.share.com**
Jumbo Shareware and Freeware: **http://www.jumbo.com/**
Software Library: **http://www.hotfiles.com/index.html**
UK Shareware: **http://www.ukshareware.com/**
US National Center for Supercomputing Applications: **http://www.ncsa.uiuc.edu/SDG/Software**

Every effort has been made to trace the copyright holders of the material in this book. If any rights have been omitted, the publishers offer their sincere apologies and will rectify this in any subsequent editions, following notification.

PHOTOGRAPHS

Cover (and p.4) Gateway P5-200 Multimedia PC - photograph reproduced with permission from Gateway 2000.
p.3 Box shots reprinted with permission from Microsoft Corporation.
p.10 With thanks to Emma Lee.
p.39 MIDI keyboard with permission from Yamaha.
p.44 Mona Lisa photograph reprinted courtesy of e.t.archive/Louvre, Paris.
p.54 Virtual Reality photograph - the latest, high-tech computer entertainment - courtesy of Cybermind UK Ltd.
p.56 Epson GT-5000 scanner: photograph courtesy of EPSON (UK) Ltd.
Fuji DX-7 digital camera: photograph reprinted with permission from Fuji Photo Film (UK) Ltd.
p.57 Cat photograph courtesy of Joan Andrews, Info Arts, USA.
Girl swimming and girl smiling: photographs from DIAMAR Interactive Corp.
p.59 Morph image courtesy of New Line Cinema/Ronald Grant Archive.

SCREEN SHOTS

Usborne Publishing Ltd. has taken every care to ensure that instructions contained in this book are accurate and suitable for their intended purpose. However, the publishers are not responsible for the content of, and do not sponsor, any Web site not owned by them, including those listed below, nor are they responsible for any exposure to offensive or inaccurate material which may appear on the Web.

Windows 95, Office, PowerPoint, Flight Simulator 98, Microsoft Agent: screen shots reprinted with permission from Microsoft Corporation. Microsoft and Microsoft Windows are registered trademarks of Microsoft Corporation in the US and other countries.
http://www.microsoft.com/
Cover: Fractal image courtesy of Paul Carlson, e-mail pjcarlsn@ix.netcom.com.
http://sprott.physics.wisc.edu/carlson.htm
http://fractal.mta.ca/fractals/carlson/
p.25 Kristy Shanks, owner of Kweb Design **(http://www.kwebdesign.com)**, has a personal page devoted to children's desktop graphics **(http://www.kwebdesign.com/kdesk/)**.
p.39 SimTunes image with permission from Maxis.
http://www.maxis.com
p.42 With thanks to Freezone.
http://freezone.com
p.43 YAHOOLIGANS! and the YAHOO! logo are trademarks of YAHOO!, Inc. All rights reserved.
http://www.yahooligans.com/
LYCOS logo ©Lycos, Inc. Used with permission.
http://www.lycos.com
Excite, WebCrawler, the Excite Logo and the WebCrawler Logo are trademarks of Excite, Inc., and may be registered in various jurisdictions. Excite screen display copyright 1995-1997 Excite, Inc.
http://www.excite.com/
http://webcrawler.com/
DIGITAL, AltaVista and the AltaVista logo are trademarks or service marks of Digital Equipment Corporation. Used with permission.
http://www.altavista.digital.com/
Tiger image reprinted with permission from Jon S. Berndt.
http://www.hal-pc.org/~jsb/tigers.html
p.44 The White House for Kids
http://www.whitehouse.gov/WH/kids/html/home.html
Hong Kong photograph with permission from the Hong Kong Tourist Association.
http://www.hkta.org/
Satellite image courtesy of Kochi University, Japan.
http://www.is.kochi-u.ac.jp/weather/index.en.html
p.45 Club-Z images reproduced with thanks to Club-Z magazine.
http://www.club-z.com/index.html
Kidz Magazine images reproduced with permission.
http://www.thetemple.com/KidzMagazine
Hotdog Express © Sausage Software
http://www.sausage.com/
Hyperlink with permission from YAHOO! Inc. All rights reserved.
E-PALS logo with permission from Freezone.
http://www.freezone.com/epals
Mailing list screen shot courtesy of Liszt.
http://www.liszt.com/
p.50 The Realm, courtesy of CUC Software International Ltd.
http://www.realmserver
Krazy Kids Collection with thanks to Emery Wang, Havana Street.
http://www.havanastreet.com
p.51 Children's Software Web page with thanks to Grace Sylvan.
http://www.gamesdomain.com/tigger/
Freezone Chat Box with thanks to Freezone.
http://chat.freezone.com
p.54 SimTown with permission from Maxis.
http://www.maxis.com
MicroWorlds is a trademark of Logo Computer Systems Inc.
http://www.lcsi.ca
p.56 Fractal images courtesy of Paul Carlson, e-mail pjcarlsn@ix.netcom.com.
http://sprott.physics.wisc.edu/carlson.htm
http://fractal.mta.ca/fractals/carlson/
Test Fractal Generator: Chris Seidel, University of California at Berkeley.
http://zenith.berkeley.edu/seidel/Frac/
p.57 Adobe® PhotoDeluxe with permission. Adobe and Adobe PhotoDeluxe are trademarks of Adobe Systems Incorporated.
p.58 QuarkXpress screen shot:
Quark, Inc. All Rights Reserved.
http://www.quark.com
p.59 Morph, courtesy of Gryphon Software Corporation, Copyright 1996.
http://mirror.gryphonsw.com/morph/faq.html#Demos

First published in 1998 by Usborne Publishing Ltd, Usborne House, 83-85 Saffron Hill, London EC1N 8RT, England. Printed in Spain.